THE H[...]
AND OTHE[...]

THE HEROINE
AND OTHER STORIES

D. Jayakanthan

Translated from Tamil
by
Deepalakshmi J.
❈
With a Foreword
by
Ambai

NIYOGI
BOOKS

Published by

NIYOGI BOOKS

Block D, Building No. 77,
Okhla Industrial Area, Phase-I,
New Delhi-110 020, INDIA
Tel: 91-11-26816301, 26818960
Email: niyogibooks@gmail.com
Website: www.niyogibooksindia.com

Text © Mrs V. Gnanambikai

Editor: K.E. Priyamvada
Design: Shraboni Roy
Cover image: Original painting by S. Elayaraja

ISBN: 978-81-933935-9-8
Publication: 2017

This is a work of fiction. The names, characters and incidents portrayed in it are the work of the author's imagination. Any resemblance to actual persons, living or dead, events or places is purely coincidental.

Printed at Niyogi Offset Pvt. Ltd., New Delhi, India

To my dear Amma;
A woman like no other.

JK — my father

His flaws were no secret, he wore them on his sleeve.
His virtues, people seldom saw with ease.
When he was petty, it was blaring and brutal.
When he was noble, it was shy and subtle.

If he was jealous, the whole world knew it;
If he admired, his own breath didn't!
His arrogance, of course, made some news;
If he was humble, nobody ever got a clue.

All at once, a saint, sinner, lover;
The best of him, he kept undercover;
Those who knew him said, 'Once met,
He was a man, one could not forget...'

— Deepalakshmi J.

❋

CONTENTS

Foreword   *9*

The Heroine   13

The Crucifixion   32

The Pervert   40

The Pallbearers   51

The Guilty   59

It's Only Words   65

Beyond Cognizance   77

New Horizons   81

A Friend Indeed   98

The Truth   113

The Masquerade   126

Translator's Note   *158*

Acknowledgements   *159*

Foreword

Putting the Human Being in the Centre

My generation grew up with some very fine writers but we always felt that Jayakanthan was one of us and that he spoke for us. He was JK to us. We romanticized his unconventional life and writing. We loved him and also hated him at times, for we did not want him to have any of the failings of an ordinary writer. He never asked us to put him up on a pedestal but we did and then occasionally when he fell down, we felt he had betrayed us. We felt that we could criticize him, as much as we admired him, for his stories — with people we saw in everyday life — made us feel that he was as simple or as complicated as those characters we felt close to. I don't know about others, but as someone who grew up in Bengaluru away from Tamil Nadu, for me JK was the rebel I dreamed of becoming. And that is how I imagined him till I had two encounters with him.

In 1964 I came to Madras Christian College (MCC) to do my MA. The college's Tamil Department, at one point, organized a debate on the topic of whether there should be co-education or not. JK was invited as the chief guest. I was not a participant but when one boy after the other went up on the stage and began to talk of girls as detractors, enticers and seducers, commenting on the way girls dress and behave, I lost my cool, took permission to say a few words and blasted the boys who spoke of girls in this manner. When it was his turn to give the address, JK said that such fights on the stage seemed very uncultured and that debates must be done with finesse. On the return that evening, when I got into the electric train from Tambaram, JK was in the same compartment. I could have spoken to him and he would have probably not minded chatting. But I was too angry with him for calling me uncultured. Within a few months JK was giving a talk in George Town and since I happened to be there I attended it. He got into a big argument with a person, probably from the DMK, who used rather uncouth language and began to shout, ridiculing the actor MGR, saying he wore a wig, and used some abusive language. I came back to the hostel and had the impudence and temerity to write and ask him if he was a schizophrenic for he had said in the college it was uncultured to fight on the stage and he had done something worse than that—he had used abusive language. Of course, I got no reply. But on another occasion a few months later when I attended another talk of his, I was sitting right at the back and was the only woman in the audience. After the event, when I was walking away, JK called out to me. 'Aren't you the one who wrote me that letter?' he asked. 'Yes, but you didn't reply,' I said. 'I am not schizophrenic; it is just that sometimes we get emotional and get overwhelmed,' he said and smiled. It was a kind of apology. Many years later when he had been invited to speak at the Jawaharlal Nehru University, he saw me in the audience and came up to me and asked, 'Aren't you the same MCC girl?' I was quite amazed at his memory. But in the intervening years he had written a lot that had both angered and won my admiration. I had a chip on my shoulder about at least one story and the sequels he had written.

In November 1966, when his *Agni Pravesam* (The Fire Test) was published, I had just turned 22. The story was considered a very bold one, for it is about a young college student coming back home on a rainy day, taking a lift from a rich man with a posh car and getting seduced by him. She comes back home and narrates the whole incident to her mother, who initially reacts with anger but later gives her an oil bath and tells her that the water poured on her had purified her. A group of us thought that the story fell short of being really radical if the girl had to be even metaphorically purified. What had she done wrong? And where was the need for this mock fire test recalling the fire test Sita was subjected to? And why was the story named *Agni Pravesam* emphasizing that the girl had undergone a metaphorical version of fire test? We were furious. But the stories that came as responses to this 'bold' story, with terrible punishments meted out to the girl with her actually burning in fire, told us that, maybe, the time had not come for even JK to write that a girl can get furious about seduction but need not be destroyed by it. Not that we were willing to forgive him for the sequels, and the film that followed sometime later made us even more furious, for JK was striving to prove that Ganga, the heroine, was pure.

The JK one could engage with, maybe, had changed over the years, for during his stay in JNU there were hardly any debates with him. Not even about some of the wonderful stories of his that we liked, such as *Kokila Enna Seythuvittaal?* (What Had Kokila Done?), *Karunaiyinal Alla* (Not out of Sympathy) and the novels *Oru Manithan, Oru Veedu, Oru Ulagam; Parisukku Po* and many other stories, some of which had been written at the time when we idolized him and which are included in this collection. He was already an icon who had won the Sahitya Akademi Award in 1972, at the age of 38, and who had said that the Akademi had honoured itself by awarding him! Jayakanthan lived to write many controversial stories, never failing to inspire many generations of youngsters and fans who always were around him. There were stories about the 'darbar' he held on the terrace of his house, but he was always surrounded by men.

I often wonder which stories of his I would choose, if I were asked to put together a collection of his work. Some of the stories I definitely would have chosen are not in this collection but then this is a collection put together by his daughter, who not only saw him differently as a person, but also saw his stories differently. She is the daughter who sang for him even when she was leaving the house in a hurry and he told her to sing Bharati's *Ninnai Charanadainthaen Kannamma* (I have taken refuge in you). There is a beautiful photograph of Jayakanthan standing bare-bodied in a lungi and little Deepalakshmi looking up at him and he looking tenderly at her. I think that closeness must have made her choose the stories in this collection differently from how I would have. These stories are about complexities in a vast spectrum of relationships; about defiance and succumbing and about human frailties and strength. There are some extraordinary women and men in these stories — women who are not afraid to throw a man out of the house when betrayed, women who stand by one another against an autocratic man in the family and reduce him to pulp, women who can wail for the dead child of another, men who can cry unashamedly and also men who can define friendships. These are stories that present the range of JK's writing from a very different perspective. These are stories which Deepalakshmi's discerning eye and her heart that understood JK for what he was, have chosen for their nuances and subtleties and for themes that can never fade away over time. Very competently translated, not straying away from the original, and yet not getting caught in just the words of the original, the stories come alive as much as the original Tamil ones, which belonged to a different period but are relevant for all times. I can only say that had JK been alive, he would have probably asked Deepalakshmi to come close to him, caressed her head and told her to sing for him, *Ninnai Charanadainthaen Kannamma* in her evocative voice. And Deepalakshmi would have obliged her father.

Ambai

THE HEROINE

For the past 15 minutes, Sitaraman is glued to the mirror, engrossed in the all-important task of setting stylish waves on his neatly brushed hair.

The room smells heavily of hairspray, whitening cream, perfume, deodorant, and the like. All of his various grooming products are scattered helter-skelter over the little dressing table, in the midst of which lies his shaving set, just-used, unwashed, with the lather still on it.

He who spends over half an hour to groom himself has neither the time nor the patience to clean his shaving set. He doesn't need to. To dutifully perform all those tasks and more, lives Madhuram, who now stands in the doorway watching him.

Madhuram is inherently proud of her husband about a lot of things.

Every morning, as she wakes him up with his bed-coffee, she feels a glint of pride about his over-sleeping!

Having finished all the other household chores, when she piles up his barely-worn shirts to wash, she feels an amused pride as she fishes out a soaked cigarette packet from one of its pockets, imagining his impish grin, if he were around.

She hands him a new handkerchief everyday as he leaves for work; Ah! His sheepish look when asked about the one she gave the previous day; she is delightfully proud of that as well!

One wonders what could be the secret behind her relentless hard work and cheerful servitude towards her utterly irresponsible husband — a father of two daughters, at that.

As it is no secret if it gets past the soul it lurks within, only Madhuram knows why. Yes, one doubts even Sitaraman is aware of it. Had he even the slightest sensibility or wisdom about it, could he display such selfish indifference towards all that she cheerfully and selflessly does for him?

However, Madhuram wouldn't hear of his alleged indifference. 'He's always been like that!' she would reassure herself. His looks, stride, way of talking — all carry a unique sense of style that appears to be conceit but it isn't! After all, doesn't she know him the best?!

That Sitaraman is very popular as a happy-go-lucky chap among his colleagues is not because they know all about his wife. Yes, they like to call him 'Hero Sitaraman', for he performs in all the plays at his office recreation club. And, of course, he always plays the 'hero' and hence the name. Nobody has ever questioned if he's worthy of the role. Contrarily, everyone including himself believes that he's the only one so qualified!

They hail him that blessed with such good looks and luck, he's sure to land a meaty 'hero' role in the movies someday.

So Sitaraman, with a high-and-mighty air that his mere presence adorns the office, sits at his desk doing practically nothing. He gets away with shirking work, joking and laughing the whole day, while his colleagues slog their backs off, listening to him, giggling, bewitched by his charm.

Even bachelors envy and wonder how Sitaraman, a father of two kids, is able to pull off such a fine lifestyle that includes expensive clothes, movie-going, and exorbitant spending.

Little do they know that it's only because Sitaraman is a family man, married to a woman like Madhuram that he's able to live with such luxury that they are unable to afford, though they are single.

Of course, they have no means to realize this. It doesn't even matter if they did not. And according to Madhuram, even Sitaraman need not; however, Sitaraman, for the sake of his own soul, surely ought to have realized it?

But our hero Sitaraman is oblivious and totally indifferent towards everything including his job, family, wife, and even life per se. His only object in life is that imminent 'hero role' that is sure to come his way.

Therefore, grooming himself with utmost care, he goes to work and sits at his desk, only to collect his unearned pay every month, waiting for the 'movie chance'. Haven't many people been lucky that way? His eyes shine with a constant glimmer of absolute arrogance.

And so, the stenographer Kamala, captivated by those handsome eyes, recently played the well-matched heroine for this 'hero'.

Just as today, Madhuram was ecstatic to watch them both together on the stage, playing hero and heroine.

Stepping back from the mirror to admire his looks, now complete with his silk shirt unbuttoned at the top, revealing a gold chain and sweeping trousers that carelessly brush over his glossy shoes, he catches sight of Madhuram standing in a corner of the room, wiping sweat and soot off her face and drying her wet hands with her saree pallu.

Seeing that he has noticed her, she smiles at him through the reflection. Approaching him with the same smiling face, she says in a kind voice: 'Listen, this month onwards, I am arranging a lunch-service for you. You are eating only breakfast before leaving for work. Having done that, if you lunch out daily at random places, what happens to your health?' He hardly seems to be listening, though he brings both his hands forward, placing them on her shoulders, and looks sharply into her eyes; and quite unusually, he seems lost in some deep thought.

'Why are you looking at me that way?' says Madhuram, looking down and blushing.

'Hmm, you were saying something? I was not listening,' he asks disinterestedly, hesitant to reveal his actual thoughts.

'Oh, what were you thinking so deeply about? Any new play in which you're acting?' chuckles Madhuram. As he shakes his head, the curly locks gently brush his forehead. Gazing fondly, Madhuram explains. 'Why should you spoil your health eating out every day? I have made arrangements for a lunch-service. Starting tomorrow, you'll have your lunch brought to your workplace. How about that? I have done right, haven't I?' She doesn't expect him to go into raptures, though. He, who couldn't care less, replies, 'What's the big deal about lunch, do whatever…' and brushes the matter aside. However, agitated about something else, his arms still around her neck, he addresses her in his sweetest manner, 'Madhuram…'

'What do you want?' she asks him lovingly; he smiles in reply.

Madhuram is bewildered at this dilly-dallying, which is quite unlike him. He usually pays her no heed as he hurries out, whistling to himself.

Sitaraman does not reply, but turns around in thoughtful silence, retrieves his wallet, and opens it. That's when he remembers his salary, which he ought to have handed to her as early as the previous day. She takes the cash he hands her and counts — 50 rupees.

'What's this? Where's the rest of your pay?' only her eyes question him, at which he smiles. She smiles back, satisfied too! That's it. The issue is resolved then and there.

Can one run an entire household relying on such a husband's earnings?

Madhuram's mother had left her this house when she passed away. Madhuram has kept the front portion for themselves and has let out the rear portions on rent. She also keeps a couple of cows and sells milk to her tenants. She never minds any of the hardships in bringing up her two little girls and this husband of hers, and deems it her own pleasure; however she often wonders what he does with his salary — all of 170 rupees. She also consoles herself and forgives everything with the lame excuse, 'Oh, men have their own expenses!' Nevertheless, is she not obliged to make him realize his faults, albeit in a subtle way?

'This is why I tell you — eating out is a waste of money, as well as spoils your health. From the day you began eating out, you have gone down half in weight. From tomorrow, I am sending over your lunch-carrier for sure.' As she reiterates the matter again, he loses patience and yells: 'Alright, alright! I heard you. I'll eat any damned thing you send. Shan't go out to any damned place to eat; happy?' He leaves.

Madhuram's eyes fill with tears at the thought that he misunderstood her good intentions and that she has angered him, just as he leaves for work.

But surprisingly, Sitaraman, who left in a huff, stops for a moment at the doorway. Composing himself in a second, he turns around and sees Madhuram with her head hung and eyes wet.

Sitaraman goes to her and holding her in a tight embrace and asks, 'Hey, are you upset?'

Madhuram is now even more perplexed. 'Oh, why should I be?' she smiles, her eyelashes still wet. She realizes that her husband is beating around the bush only to get something out of her, but also wonders why. She stares at the 50 rupees in her hand.

'Madhu, Madhu, won't you come in, I have something to tell you,' putting on a false expression of cheer, he ushers her back inside the room with his arm around her. The cheer dies down though, as soon as he sits down on the bed.

'What is the matter? Tell me,' hands on her waist, she asks him. She senses the notes clenched in her fist. She is almost sure that he wants them back and if so, she is not going to refuse.

'Nothing...I have been thinking it over...it's good for you too in a way...' he falters, unable to bring himself to say what he really wants to. Watching his plight, Madhuram sits beside him with a reassuring smile.

'What are you hemming and hawing about...huh? What is it?' She turns his chin towards her. Her eyes shine with the goodwill that meant 'I shall give you whatever you ask.' Finding his head still hung, she rises to leave, affecting impatience, 'Fine, I've got work to do.'

'Stay!' he pulls her into a tight hug and brings his face close to hers, seemingly passionate. 'Madhu, do you really mean it when you always say my happiness is just as yours?' Her cheeks burn with his breath.

'Yes, what of that now? Look, your clothes are getting creased; you need to leave for work,' Madhuram, draws herself from him.

'I believe "his majesty" has exceeded his expenses beyond the limit last month,' Madhuram says to herself. 'Maybe it was just pretence giving me this money and now he wants it back, but why? Can't I do without this 50 rupees? I can manage somehow along with my other hardships.

I feel sorry for him begging and fussing like this. But what does he do with so much money? I wonder!' Though her mind wanders this way and that, thanks to her strict traditional upbringing, she firmly believes that a man, and a husband at that, is above such scrupulous interrogation about money matters, and so remains silent with a forlorn smile.

He goes on speaking, his lips caressing her earlobes: 'I have a favour to ask of you. It's not just for me, which is why I hesitate so much. You know Kamala, my colleague, the stenographer?' His voice breaks at these words.

'Who? *Your heroine*, Kamala?'Madhuram asks scathingly.

'Hmm, as though he is thrifty enough, he is also up to charity, I believe. Such vanity,' she murmurs to herself. Meanwhile, she also expected a reply when she emphasized on the words 'your heroine'.

The other day when they returned home from the play, he asked her playfully, 'So, what do you think of my heroine, eh?'

'Ah, your heroine indeed!' she pretended to be annoyed.

'Hey! Only in the play. Aren't you my real heroine?' This is what she wants to hear again.

Sitaraman distractedly nods his head, though. 'Yes, she's the one. She'll come home this afternoon, here! Whatever she asks of you, you must give wholeheartedly. Will you? She trusts you a lot. She'd be greatly indebted to you for this favour you'd be granting her. Poor thing, she is a very good girl; has nobody for herself.' As Sitaraman went on so compassionately, Madhuram finds it distasteful. She does not like it. She actually gets slightly irritated.

'Okay, okay, let her come. Aren't you getting late?' she hastily tries to distract him.

'Oh yes! Goodbye now,' Sitaraman takes her leave.

Madhuram is unable to put things together. She tries to envisage the childish face of Kamala who performed with her husband. 'Why should this man be so concerned about lending her money?' As her mind deduces the various possible explanations for this, she rebukes herself saying, 'Gosh, how could I be so unfairly judgemental about a woman?'

That's Madhuram's disposition. Be it her husband or her household problems or her children's disputes, she easily finds an excuse for everything. For how can she spend all her day dwelling on such thoughts? Oh, in about an hour both her little girls will be back from school, hungry! All her husband's and children's clothes soaked in soapy water are waiting to be washed…the cooking pot is boiling in the kitchen…the cows need to be fed…how many chores to be done—she is both stressed and excited about completing all these tasks in front of her. Immediately, she forgets everything, and as the very first task, she picks up her husband's neglected shaving set and runs into the bathroom to clean it.

After two in the afternoon she gets a little rest. In that short while, less than an hour, she spreads her pallu on the drawing room floor and lies down near the back door, so as to enjoy the good breeze from the backyard. Before long, she'd be satisfied. She'd wake up, wash her face and sit down to comb her hair. If not for then, she can never find time to comb her hair at all. 'So what?' you ask. Well, how much ever a woman bustles with the oddest of chores, she ought not to look dirty and shabby when her husband comes back home; it is a bad omen for the family. Therefore, she would finish prettying herself up by as early as three in the afternoon.

So what does this mean? Does she expect his arrival starting 3 pm? The flower seller comes at 4 pm. That's her time. And she has two little girls for whom she buys flowers too. But it's not true that she buys flowers only for their sake, as she claims!

Around dusk, she comes and stands at the front door, every now and then. She wants him to be surprised. 'Is this the same woman that I saw with shabby hair and dirty clothes in the morning?'

He would mostly pay her no notice as he enters. She would be unperturbed though. Sometimes he would smile at her decking up. She would not understand the scorn behind it.

This afternoon as she lays the mirror against the wall and begins combing her hair, she parts her hair and looks keenly at the grey lock on her forehead. 'Well, it gets hidden when you apply oil and braid your hair, doesn't it?'

She arrives just when Madhuram is oiling her hair. Anxious that the 'heroine Kamala' should not see her grey hair, Madhuram hastily picks up the comb and goes inside the bedroom and starts tying it into a bun. She asks herself though: 'Why? What if she sees my grey hairs? Why am I so concerned that she shouldn't?'

'Am I feeling insecure that the perfectly suited heroine would mock at me, his unsuitable real life heroine?'

Kamala enters. 'Come dear; the last I saw you was at that play. Why don't you come home often? Please sit down. I'll be right there.' Carefully pressing down her front locks several times, Madhuram walks back into the front hall smiling amiably.

'Oh, why do you stand? Please sit down,' offering her a seat on the two-seater bamboo sofa, she sits down opposite her on a single seater. That's her usual hostess seat.

Seating herself, Kamala looks around, 'Where are the children?'

'They're not yet back from school.'

'Oh, the little one has started school too, has she?'

'Yes, just this year. One day she'd go happily, throw tantrums the other!' Madhuram smiles. There is a dearth of conversation for about a second. Madhuram quickly covers it by continuing to talk about her younger child. 'If she doesn't go to school, she behaves in such an unruly manner at home. My elder one is so docile. Goodness knows how this one is so naughty! She hates to put anything on. The moment she's back from school, she pulls off her dress and underpants and runs around the house stark naked. I've even tried thrashing her, but to no avail!' Madhuram vivaciously describes her child's antics.

'Oh she's just a child,' Kamala now retrieves a biscuit tin and two big chocolate packets from her handbag and places them on the sofa.

Madhuram is perplexed. 'Why should she who's in need of money herself, spend so much on these?'

As usual she makes an excuse. 'She is visiting us for the first time and felt she had to get something.' She still asks,' What's the need to get all this? Waste of money.'

'Oh Akka! Must you talk as though to a stranger?' Kamala asks Madhuram with an air of intimacy.

As Madhuram smiles good-humouredly at Kamala, she takes in her attire, make-up, hairstyle, and scrutinizes them all just as a goldsmith would inspect a gold ornament. She puts the kettle on and returns.

Waiting in vain for Kamala to speak, Madhuram begins herself, 'Just this morning he was saying…'

'Oh, what did he say?' Kamala asks startled.

'Oh, nothing. Only that you'll come to visit. And well, he also said you have nobody. I wanted to ask him then and there, but there wasn't time. Who do you live with? Which is your native place? If not parents, you must have some kin for sure?' Madhuram piles up all her questions as one.

Kamala does not answer at once. She just sits there head down; her head lowers and lowers until the nerves on her neck swell and shiver; her earlobes turn pink. As she raises her head again, her eyes are reddened with tears.

Madhuram panics. 'Have I asked something amiss?' She draws near Kamala and kindly asks her, 'Why are you upset, dear?'

'I came to ask you of a favour, thinking of you as my own sister.' Choking with unsaid emotions, Kamala bites her lip, unable to say anymore.

'I lost my parents at an early age and went through school, living with many hardships at my uncle's. Somehow having secured a job, I earned my freedom from that hell. But how long can I stay at a hostel and live a companionless life?' As Kamala asks this with her nose quivering with tears, Madhuram clearly empathizes with her situation.

'Why? You could get married, make your own family and live like a queen. What are you lacking in? You are not even an illiterate like me. Is this what you are upset about?' she comforts Kamala.

Kamala lets out a sigh. 'Marriage and stuff happens to only those with kith and kin or responsible guardians. I have none. In these 26 years of life, I got used to this fact and had resolved to live my life all alone. But he has been the only one who showed this orphan affection and has done a lot for me—Mr Sitaraman.' As Kamala said this and stopped speaking, the two women look at each other carefully.

Madhuram has a sudden premonition, a firm belief; it is not evident in her facial expressions. Undiscernible, it nails her as a statue and she now looks at Kamala with piercing eyes. Kamala on her part, realizes that Madhuram had understood her intentions in coming here, and gapes back at her.

'What if she refuses me? What if she affronts me and drives me away? And what if she calls for justice and insults me in front of a huge crowd?' With panic building up within her steadily, Kamala lets out a huge sob and drops her head on Madhuram's palms, wailing.

Now, Madhuram asks nothing but continues to stare into the now empty space as Kamala has moved and fallen into her arms.

Weeping bitterly, Kamala grabs Madhuram's hands tightly and finally manages to say: 'I beg you to share your life with me, Akka.'

Holding tears as a shield, she has sliced Madhuram's heart with a mighty sword.

'You must show this orphan a way. My reputation depends on you. Please forgive my betrayal towards you and save me. Your child and my unborn one are but the same, Akka!'

Now, she has drawn the sword and brought it down heavily, one more time. Madhuram shuts her eyes and bites her lips, mustering all the courage in her heart to bear this.

'I'll never forget this as long as I live. I shall remain indebted to you and your family, I mean our family…'

Madhuram cuts her in… 'Enough Kamala! That's enough. Oh my God! This is unbearable!' Wounded beyond measure, Madhuram falls on the sofa shaking her head, shivering with agony.

Then, for at least half an hour, Madhuram stays still, her eyes shut.

Having said everything, and expecting Madhuram's consent and reply, Kamala sits there trembling with fear and anticipation.

She feels deeply about Madhuram's plight as well. Contrary to her fears, Madhuram has neither yelled nor cursed her, and so she is guilt-ridden for having broken such a kind heart. She is overcome with sobs now.

Thus sobbing quietly for a long time, she comes near Madhuram and nudges her, 'Akka! Akka!'

Madhuram opens her eyes and sits up, her expression completely nonchalant, and her face clear. Her resolute eyes are now as red as rose petals.

'Why are you crying *ma*? Be brave!' with those words Madhuram rises and goes inside the bedroom. She wishes to be alone for a while. Her eyes are fixed on the bed and his clothes on the coat stand.

As she paces up and down the room with her hands behind her back, Kamala keeps glancing at her.

Madhuram stands in front of the mirror and scans herself; at the same spot where her 'darling' husband stands and grooms himself every day. The grey locks have escaped their hidden place and protrude out, having been combed in a hurry. Her face is wrinkled, her body flabby, and she looks much older than her age.

'How good he looks? Just as I had seen years ago?' She now steals a glance at Kamala sitting in the hall. 'Yes, she's the right match for him. I have become old! But how? How can I, who's younger look older than him? It's not age that has aged me but my stupidity.' She gnashes her teeth in anger.

She has lost her entire life about him. As she stood admiring him, taking care of his youthfulness, she failed to realize her own youth leaving her.

She thinks about all of that now. What is now gnawing at her is not the fact that another woman has stolen her husband, but that she has been so naïve to trust a falsehood and has lost all the sweetest years of life in wasted labour and hardships. This now trickles as the bitterest of truths. She stands there staring into vacant space, becoming almost hysterical.

She keeps sighing and sighing. She has no words to speak what she felt. Yet, she is saying to herself: 'If I bear the entire family responsibility on my head, then it's no wonder my hair has greyed. Was I like him, without a care in the world? As I stood between every difficulty and him, of course, he could look like a hero all his life. Yes, I was happy thinking about him. I had no time to think about even myself. But he has apparently needed more than me. Ah, what a huge betrayal? What a shameful exploitation? What a nauseating life I have lived? Oh, dear Amma...I'd be damned if I am to see his face again.' She keeps talking to herself.

Presently she comes to Kamala, looks at her with pity and says: 'Kamala, what can I do for your fate? You are asking for a share in my life! But what kind of life have I lived? Have I really lived? Please, I entreat you with all my heart. Kindly take the whole of it! For 15 years, I have lived with him and it was all for naught. Oh, what not have I done and faced! It's alright. You must run along now! Please go tell him there's no room for him in this house anymore. If I even so much as glance at that face, I might scream and die. Betrayal is not as painful as having to face the smile of the traitor. That is hell. My kids and I are not dependent on anybody. You too please understand that. I may have lived for 15 years trusting him, but not a day relying on him; nobody can. He is so! You please hurry up and go tell him that he need not bother coming back. Go! As for your fate, what can I do, tell me? This heroine has had enough. Doesn't he need another?' With these words, Madhuram walks away.

The determination in her voice and the composure in her words make it evident to Kamala that Madhuram's decision is not impulsive. Head hung, she's fidgeting with her fingernails. Madhuram stands tall and looks at her, eyes filled with sympathy.

She remembers her pleading words, 'Please show a way for this orphan,' and '...I consider you as my own sister...'

'Kamala, you have counted on me as your own sister and asked me for guidance. How could I do that? My mother was alive then. When I was stubborn that I would marry this man, she tried a lot to dissuade me. But I paid heed to none of her good advice.' Madhuram sheds tears in memory of her mother.

'Maybe she foresaw all this and left this house for me and not her other children. It is this house that takes care of me and my children, Kamala. All the care I ought to have bestowed on this house, and the love on those two cows, I have sinfully wasted on him.' At these words, Madhuram roars in a sudden rage. 'This is MY house. No stranger can dare cross its threshold.'

Kamala is astounded.

Madhuram quickly retreats, fearing she might blurt out anything too personal, if she stood there any longer.

Kamala's gaze is now fixed on the shut door of Madhuram's room. She buries her face in her hands and sobs bitterly. Why does she sob now? For her own fate?

She recollects Madhuram's strong words: 'This heroine has had enough; the nightmare is over.' She is awed at Madhuram's courage for having disowned him with such gumption. 'Oh! What a woman!' Kamala's chest heaves with pride.

The sheer determination of this woman, who unlike her, has neither the security of education nor a profession, gives Kamala undue confidence that she doesn't need to beg anything from anyone.

'Should I complicate my life anymore?' His face looms in front of her eyes, as if it were the answer. She is now able to clearly discern the abandon in those eyes.

'Such a good wife, all her hard work, her love, her benevolence— he has ruthlessly exploited and what has he done to her in return?' Analysing him thus as a third person would, Kamala is filled with a sudden loathing, which grows rapidly into a venomous hatred.

Yes, she has not loved him for her rational reasons; it was a weakness. In these few months of acquaintance, she herself has unearthed thousands of reasons to despise him wholeheartedly.

'Well,' said Madhuram. 'What a nauseating life I have lived!' The depth and reason behind those words open her own eyes as well.

Kamala raises her head and sits up. There shines a new glint of hope in her own eyes.

'Hmm, if a mother of two is so confident to stand on her own, why can't I with my yet-to-be born child? And even if we suffer, can this man be my knight-in-arms?'

'This heroine has had enough too...' Biting her lips with grit, she opens her handbag, takes out a pen and paper and starts writing a letter.

Sitaraman stands waiting in the park until seven, for Kamala. She was supposed to meet him at six with the 'good news'. However he is unperturbed that she hasn't turned up. He brims with utmost confidence and bravado that nothing contrary to his wishes can ever happen in life!

A wife to earn money, a wife to serve as a doormat—with these imminent selfish desires, he arrives home at eight, whistling gaily as usual. He is doubly excited that there will be two wives waiting to receive him home.

However, as he reaches the hall, he can neither find Kamala nor Madhuram but only his two daughters. His eldest, Uma is sitting on the sofa doing her homework. Little one, Latha stands behind her sister, playing pranks and pulling her plaits. On one side of the sofa, biscuits lie scattered.

Sitaraman feels kicked right in his chest as the kitchen door slams shut as he steps in. He walks towards the kitchen.

Gently he calls out to her, 'Madhu! Madhu.' She is leaning over the shut double doors, her frame visible through the narrow opening between them.

Her voice sounds loud and clear 'If you had any sense of honour, get out of my house. There is no room for you here. This is MY house.'

'Madhu, open the door please, I tell you,' her husband implores, as though tearfully.

'No, if I so much as get a glimpse of your face, no please! I don't want the tag of a woman who spat on her husband's face.'

Sitaraman feels boxed on his ears. Sweat covers his face; he is facing the biggest ever disaster in his life!

A sudden gush of anger rises through him!

'Hey, what are you talking, woman? What will you do if I refuse to leave?' he kicks at the kitchen door.

Madhuram laughs hysterically; her laugh sounds like the shattering of a heavy glass vessel. In the midst of her mirth, she says. 'Good, you stay. Those two children ought to have either their father or mother. By all means you be,' saying this she tugs off the clothes line in the kitchen. Sitaraman starts panicking. His hands and knees begin shaking. He visualizes what could now happen behind the closed doors. Every moment that he dallies anymore, that rope could tighten a bit more around her neck!

He screams in sheer terror: 'Madhuram, I am leaving! I am leaving! Here…I am leaving right now!' he shouts, banging both his hands on the door.

'Leave!' Madhuram lashes back with utter disregard and strikes his hand with the rope. Sitaraman fully senses her anger and disgust in that blow.

Madhuram on her part realizes that Sitaraman has not panicked because of his love for her, but because he would be forced to bear the responsibility of the two children after her death. '*Chee*!' She shudders with revulsion.

Finally, against her sweet nature of always finding an excuse for his behaviour, she fully comes to terms with all his failings in their true colours.

Sitaraman runs to his room, hurriedly packs his suitcases and stops for a moment in the hall. Finding a letter in the letterbox, he puts his suitcases down, retrieves it and starts reading.

Both the children, blissfully unaware of what's happening around them, are happily eating the biscuits and chocolates. Uma takes a bite out of a big chocolate bar, places it by her side and continues to write in her note book. Latha sneaks up beside her and takes a bite out of the same chocolate. Uma picks it up saying '*Chee*, your drool! I don't want it anymore,' and hands it back to her little sister.

Little Latha blinks at the chocolate in her hand. She learns that her sister had rejected it, because one is not supposed to eat another's leftovers. She also realizes that she has just eaten her big sister's 'drool'. She is now repulsed too.

'*Chee*…drool, I don't want it either!' She throws away the chocolate bar and spitting out the remaining bits, wipes her mouth.

The half-bitten chocolate bar falls at Sitaraman's feet. He glances at it for a second. Crumpling the letter in hand, picking up both the suitcases, he hurries out of the front door.

'Hey Uma, come here! *Appa* is going, bye bye!' calls out Latha running to the front door; Uma follows.

As Sitaraman turns to look at his kids from down the street, they wave their typical good byes, '*Appa*, ta-ta!'

Sitaraman's eyes, the eyes that always shine with a reckless abandon adorning them and making him a hero, now well up and glisten with tears.

THE CRUCIFIXION

The bus rattled noisily along the trunk road. Careful not to glance at the youth seated across from her, the young nun fixed her eyes onto the landscape outside the window; there, she saw the most wonderful sight ever.

A peasant woman, a straw bundle atop her head, stood nursing a baby latched onto her breast. The baby was already lulled to sleep. The woman pulled her saree drape over the child's head to protect it from the sun's glare as she watched the speeding bus. For a fleeting moment, her eyes met with that of the nun's. The nun, moved by what she had seen, felt a glow light up her heart. Craning her neck, she peered through the window, her blue veil fluttering in the wind. The woman noticed her and smiled. The nun nodded her head in reply.

'Hail Mary, mother of God, the Lord be with you…' her lips muttered. The peasant woman reminded her of the Virgin Mary statue that stood in the chapel of their monastery. As the woman slowly vanished from sight, the young man's face loomed again in front of her eyes.

He had been looking at her all the while—at her oval face framed by the soft blue and black veil.

The nun felt herself shudder slightly and her heart race; hurriedly she shifted her gaze back to the window.

'What?' she said to herself, 'Is he not good enough to look at? But then, all sins are attractive, indeed, wrapped in tempting packages. Human birth by itself is the mightiest of sins. Had only Adam and Eve stayed clear off the forbidden fruit, humans would have never been born. Adam and Eve were the only humans born devoid of sin but they became sinners for they disobeyed the lord. We all are the fruit of their sin. All of us, even my mother Invilata who sits here beside me; (she adopted me as a child and brought me up, an austere nun just like herself) and so is the peasant woman I just saw, and her baby, and this young man who is still staring at me! All sinners, worms born out of the forbidden fruit; venomous snakes!'

The bus was speeding on its way. As she looked back into the bus, her eyes again met the young man's for a moment, before catching sight of a small baby sitting on her mother's lap. The baby's cherubic smile went straight into her heart. The nun smiled back at the baby, who readily jumped up to her. Climbing down from her mother's lap, the child held the knees of Mother Invilata and looked up at her. The old woman was however deeply engrossed in the tiny silver cross hung from the rosary round her neck. It was her usual way. From the time she had boarded the bus two hours ago, she had been sitting quietly, her eyes fixed on the holy Christ's image engraved on the cross. Now, she looked at the child and smiled, touching its cheek in a loving gesture. The child tugged at her rosary; Mother Invilata handed the tiny pendant to the child and taught her to pray, 'C'mon little angel, say your prayers!'

The child imitated her and turned towards the younger nun, her dimpled rosy face shining with smiles. The young nun scooped up the child in her arms and hugged her close to her chest. Her heart overflowed and a lump grew in her throat. Her eyes grew moist.

'Catherine, what's the time please?' Invilata asked her, her eyes fixed on the cross again. Catherine, the younger nun, however did not hear.

She was ecstatically cuddling the child, caressing the soft cheeks with her own.

'Catherine! Catherine! Are you sleeping? Careful not to drop the child! Pray what's the time, please!'

'Mother, it's five,' Catherine replied as she put the child down. 'Say your prayers, little dear, say your prayers!' She cuddled the baby again. And then, again, her eyes fell on the man sitting opposite her. This time though, she did not shift her eyes immediately; locked by his gaze, was she in a trance now?

He should be in his mid-twenties. Tall, dark, and well-built, he had a dignified and subdued grace about him that was very intriguing. As he was seated by the window, his hair and necktie kept fluttering in the breeze. As he brushed aside a wavy lock away from his brow, he noticed her looking at him. Quite naturally, his lips gave way to a subtle smile. Catherine could not help but return that attractive smile, as though in a reflex action.

When she smiled, Catherine looked like an angel walking the earth. Her innate sweet disposition, combined with imbibed values of love for all living creatures, rendered a radiant glow to her face. 'Oh what must he think of me?' Catherine thought again. 'Is he wondering why I am thus? Will he think I am fickle and not up to celibacy? Or fallible and impulsive?' Catherine turned and looked at her mother Invilata, who sat serenely in her own world, where nothing else mattered but the tiny little cross she held. Her face had a gentle smile, and her lips occasionally murmured in prayer. Catherine compared herself with her mother and felt ashamed. She went on to count the number of confessions she had made in all her 18 years of life.

'Mother?'

'Yes, Catherine?' Invilata turned to face her daughter.

'Mother, have you ever made any grave confessions?'

'Why yes, of course, child! We are all sinners, after all. But an honest confession to the lord fetches us atonement. The Lord bears all our sins, and that's why we confess our daily sins to Him before bedtime, and get our souls cleansed. Moreover, when you confess to our Holy Father in the church, our soul gets redeemed and we are pardoned. Our father prays for us; I have committed many a sin myself,' she added with a sigh.

Catherine was surprised. 'Could Invilata have had the same feelings as I am presently going through?'

'Catherine! I must have been as old as you are now. I had a weird dream — that I was getting married! What a sinful dream indeed! I woke up and wept all night. What upset me most was that I seemed very happy in the dream. Can a nun get dreams like that? I immediately went for confession to our Father the next day; I fasted the whole day and kept praying to the Lord.'

The old woman lowered her voice and continued. 'And another time, I smacked a student in class, and she was bruised. I felt so guilty and ashamed that I confessed for that as well; there should be quite a few of such occasions.'

'Is that all? I can't even believe this!' Catherine was chagrined. 'Suppose, she is not entirely truthful?' she wondered.

'Hiding one's sins is the way of Satan. We must open our hearts and confess with a clear breast. We cannot have secrets from Him,' Invilata continued, as though having read Catherine's thoughts.

'Yes, one cannot have secrets from the Lord,' Catherine agreed. Then she took a book out of her bag and attempted to read. Her eyes once more travelled four seats forward, beside the window...

He was still looking at her. 'Oh, what a piercing look it is!' She went on to read the Bible. '... *But I say to you that everyone who looks at a woman with lustful intent has already committed adultery with her in his heart…If your right eye causes you to sin, pluck it out and throw it away. It is better to lose an organ than your whole body burning in hell.*' Catherine could read no more. She closed her eyes; the book lay open in her hands.

'Why do I get so many sinful thoughts?' she implored. 'Why has he still not got down? Is he a messenger of Satan, come to test my will? Oh, can't I stop thinking about him? Oh, Father!'

With a sudden will, she crossed herself and began praying in earnest. '…*do not bring us to the test, but deliver us from evil, Amen!*' But to no avail; as soon as her eyes opened, they went straight to meet the young man's. 'Can humans ever be free from sin? Why did the Garden of Eden created by God for Adam and Eve hold forbidden trees and snakes as well? How could humans and sins both be His creations? Is the joy borne by sins only ephemeral? Are all joys sinful? In that case, should the majority of mankind rot in hell? Why am I among the very few who fear sin like the end of the world? There, the youth sits looking at me, so ardently…how can I blame him, for I am actually no different from any other young woman!'

Catherine saw a young couple seated a few seats away. Either out of fatigue or fondness, the young pregnant wife was snuggling close to her husband, her eyes closed and her head laid on his shoulder, with a contented air. This vision roused in Catherine, a satanic notion.

'Isn't this nun's habit my only obstacle? If only I could shed it and throw myself into this young man's arms? Good lord! I am continually thinking about sins! Please pardon me!'

The bus came to a halt. A great crowd thronged about the terminal. Invilata and Catherine waited until the rest of the passengers got down, and proceeded to alight last.

A coachman came running. 'To the monastery? Please come this way, sisters,' he ushered them towards his coach.

Just then, the young man came towards them. He looked dashing in his white shirt and blue suit, against the backdrop of the beautiful setting sun. To Catherine, he clearly seemed a true messenger of Satan!

Catherine felt herself blush as she exchanged cordial smiles with him. He stepped forward and first greeted Invilata in a manner appropriate for clergywomen. Invilata greeted him back.

As he turned to Catherine and she returned his respectful greeting, she could not help choking; her eyes filled with tears. As both the nuns boarded the coach, he waved at them amiably.

Catherine waved back smiling. As the coach rattled away, he vanished from sight. Catherine's hand fell limp and her heart grew heavy.

'Catherine, who was that? I don't recognize him,' enquired Invilata.

Catherine assumed a nonchalant look and blithely lied, 'Oh, Mother! I barely recognized him either; he is the brother of one of my pupils, Isabel.'

'Oh.'

'Oh, my dear Father. Please pardon me. I have done nothing but sin all day.' However, she still kept reminiscing about his smiling face and the wave of his hand. 'Who was he? Will I ever see him again? Am I entitled to that privilege, or sin, whatever!' she yearned.

When she realized she was not even allowed to sin, she felt her heart break and mammoth sobs erupting from within. However, was she allowed to cry? No! Her veil fluttered in the breeze and covered her face. Behind the veil, she wept bitterly, trembling with her singular grief. Invilata was, of course, lost in the tiny cross in her hand, quite oblivious to anything else!

All night, Catherine stayed awake, praying for atonement for all her sins. Now and then though, she remembered the youth's face and sighed to herself. Finally she dozed off to sleep and had a most unusual dream: Invilata was carrying a huge heavy cross. Slowly her persona grew higher than the church towers. The cross that she carried over her shoulders was reduced to a small figurine in her hands. She kept smiling at it, praying gently with a divine smile on her face. The church bells rang. A hallowed beam of light fell from the heavens and enveloped Invilata. The church bells rang louder than before. Then, there was another huge cross, quite similar to the one Invilata carried. Catherine came forward in the hope of carrying it; however, try as she might, she found it so heavy and the cross wouldn't budge an inch. Panting and wanting for breath, she felt her back being whipped and she writhed in pain. Just then she heard a voice.

'Catherine, my love! My dearest Catherine!' She turned around to see the youth running towards her. Catherine left the cross and ran towards him. She fell into his extended arms and buried her face in his chest, weeping uncontrollably. He lifted her chin and kissed her on her lips. Oh, what a kiss it was!

'Is this a sin? I'd gladly be a sinner then, all my life!' and she embraced him tightly.

The church bells rang again, as loudly as before.

Catherine woke up startled, feeling terribly guilty and anguished. As she went for her morning prayers with others, she wept with all her heart. Could the tears wash away all her sins, and wipe her heart clean? Later that day, Catherine went in for confession. The reverend, in his pristine robes, smiled warmly at her; Catherine felt utterly abashed to approach him.

'Father...'

'My child!' he stooped towards her to listen.

'I am a huge sinner, father. I have sinned terribly.'

'Ah! We were born so our sins may be pardoned! The holy Christ was born not to redeem saints but the sinners. Open up and confess your sins, my child, and be forgiven.'

Catherine drew towards him. Pain wrought across her face, sobbing uncontrollably, and shuddering all over, she screamed to the utter bewilderment of the Reverend, 'Oh kind Father, my sin...my greatest sin ever...was that I grew up to be a nun!'

THE PERVERT

Facing the front gates, beneath the lights of the porch, Dr Raghavan stretched comfortably on his armchair; a Balzac novel in one hand and a gleaming cigarette in another.

It was only seven in the evening, and apparently his consultation hour; but it was pointless to stay cooped up within his office, when there were no patients to see. He would have been glad to have one of his friends to visit, but there was no sign of them either.

He had his mansion divided into his clinic to the front and his household to the rear. His cook, Raman Nair, was at work, humming a Malayalam tune to himself. Once he left, Raghavan would be left all alone with only his books for company, and he cared for little else. However, each time he had devoured one of his favorite erotica like *Loves of Casanova* or *Lady Chatterley's Lover*, he sought out his friends for a delightful discourse on the various titillating lines, which he had underlined and made a mental note of!

With this book yet unfinished, he had no purpose to call on one of them. So he sat back, took a last deep puff from his cigarette, savoured it with relish, and flicked the butt away. After a few moments of reminiscence, he sat up to read again, wiping his sooty glasses and putting them back on. In a short while, he was lost in the vivid narration of scandalizing 18th-century French affairs, with a tingling delight coming over him.

His friends, no matter how much they enjoyed his relentless discourses on sex, secretly disdained him. However, they all agreed that for a staunch bachelor of 35, his personal conduct was impeccable. A few of them had tried to spy on him for any funny behaviour and had failed. It was to be believed that Raghavan was a true gentleman after all, in every worldly sense. A few others grew tired of his unabashed and never-ending sex-talk and severed ties with him, especially after getting married. As single men, they all used to relish his talks, though.

Raghavan, however, had no qualms about his penchant for sex, or even sex per se. On the contrary, he strongly believed it was a noble and selfless exercise. He neither cared nor doubted that his talks could be scandalizing. His passion for sex rose not out of his self-centredness, but of his intense wonderment and deep wisdom about life. Therefore, however filthy or despicable his talks seemed to others, to Raghavan they evoked only a sense of elation and fulfilment.

That sex is the very foundation of life was his unswerving philosophy; his talks were all odes praising that beautiful truth; he felt no need to mask his words with unnecessary frills.

Raghavan often wondered why people were so contemptuous about a natural and beautiful emotion, repressed it with shame, and practised it as a crime; and he believed he knew why.

Sex is a subject that's never broached impersonally. People do not appreciate its beauty as the closest thing to every living being, but rather something very personal to each of them. They perceive every sexual act or description with utmost self-consciousness.

Both men and women, when beholding a sexual act, see themselves in the respective parts, nettled by their own prejudices, failing to see the broader perspective. We all love to admire our nudity in secret, but cover up in front of others. This is the essence of human hypocrisy.

These notions of Raghavan, however philosophical and elevated they might have been, earned him among his friends, the reputation of a 'pervert'. His friends began shunning him gradually, not without impacting his profession as well.

Raghavan, however, was blissfully unperturbed by any of this. As long as there was a steady supply of the kind of books he lived on, from all over the world onto libraries and book stores, he had nothing to worry.

Having just finished a chapter and feeling content, he wanted to take a break to smoke. The cigarette case beside him was empty. Before he could call out to his cook to bring a new pack, Raman Nair, the cook, came down the hallway, having finished his chores.

Mainly because they spoke different tongues, Raman Nair did not have much insight about his employer. However, he knew enough to understand that Dr Raghavan led a bohemian lifestyle. He felt pity for the young man who did not care much about himself, and only sat reading for hours together. Being a good fellow at heart, he seldom left after finishing his culinary duties, and insisted that Raghavan sit down for his meal. At times when Raghavan was engrossed in his talks or books, with utter disregard about mealtimes, Raman Nair dilly-dallied, trying to get Raghavan's attention so he could remind him to eat. However, Raghavan never got the cue and used to dismiss him for the day.

The cook had been greatly upset at times when he went to cook dinner and found the lunch untouched! So, it was only natural that he eagerly came running when called, hoping that his master was hungry.

'Dinner is ready sir, will you eat now?' he asked.

Raghavan looked up nonchalantly. For a moment, he went blank as to why he had called his cook. As he absent-mindedly fumbled with the empty cigarette case in hand, he suddenly remembered.

'No, I am not hungry. Please get me my cigarette pack from the table, and you may leave.' The clock in the hallway struck eight. Raman handed him the cigarettes and left. Raghavan lit a new one and leaned back on his chair.

As he began reading a new chapter in earnest, somebody walked in through the gates. Raghavan adjusted his spectacles and peered through them. It was dark and it was not clear who was opening the gates. Raghavan fervently hoped it was one of his friends, with whom he could freely share the forbidden delights of the book that he was reading.

Soon he found out that the visitor was not one of his friends but a woman. Though it was past his consultation hour, and none of his regular patients were women, he still asked her to be seated. He remembered seeing her before, and the preceding incident, but try as he might, he could not recollect her name. However, in an attempt to show familiarity, he enquired after her grandmother. She did not reply immediately but sat with her head down, fidgeting with her finger nails. This gave him free rein to observe her intently.

He noticed that she was even paler and more distraught than when he had met her two years ago, in grave danger. He could see that not just her health, but her whole life had been disastrous, evident from the bleached old saree she was wearing.

She discreetly wiped away the tears that fell on to the back of her palm, and lifted her head to reply, 'Grandma passed away a year ago.' Her lips trembled in sorrow.

With a huge sigh, Raghavan turned aside. He remembered the old lady who was deeply fond of her grandchild, this young woman. 'What's your name?' he asked her, without looking at her.

'Radha,' she replied, still looking down. He could recall the name at once.

'Radha,' he murmured as he turned to glance at her. She looked up at him with listless eyes. It appeared that those eyes had no room for any sentiment whatsoever. What remained of her ravaged beauty was just as poignant as the ruins of ancient monuments, and evoked nothing but sympathy. Though Raghavan had forgotten her name, he remembered her very well.

❈

A couple of years ago, Radha's grandmother had come running to him, crying bitterly and imploring him for help.

As Raghavan went along the path through which she led him, he was shocked to find the deplorable state of the pitiful slum, just next to the posh suburb in which he lived. Following the old woman, he treaded through dingy streets, leaped across puddles of sewage water, some of it splashing on to his foot, and finally made his way to a dark little hut.

The old woman borrowed a match box from next door and lit a lamp before ushering him inside. In the dim light, Raghavan saw a young woman sprawled against a wall; for a moment he wondered if it was too late. The old woman called out to the girl, 'Radha dear, look, the doctor is here,' and she started sobbing uncontrollably.

Raghavan gently asked her to be quiet, and knelt before his patient. He opened her eyelids and checked for her pulse.

'Idiotic girl. What has she done! I am so scared, my lord. You are our saviour, please help us...' the old woman began wailing. 'What happened?' Raghavan asked her.

Stifling her sobs with her saree folds, the old woman swore, 'She has poisoned herself, with this goddamn thing,' and showed him an empty aluminium tumbler.

Raghavan took the tumbler from her, examined it in the light, and then sniffed at it. He put it down and stood up. Closing his eyes, he rubbed his forehead, deep in thought.

The old woman started panicking. She fell on her knees. 'Ayya! Will my child live? Please save us, we are poor, show mercy please!' Raghavan hushed her, replaced the lamp in its stand and took out a syringe from his bag. Kindling the lamp a little further, he fished in his bag for the antidote. 'Bring me some water please.' The old woman reached out for the same aluminium tumbler. Raghavan glared at her, 'For god's sake, can't you use something else?' The poor woman realized her blunder and trembled.

'Please don't fear. Your daughter will be alright,' he said and lifted the girl's arm to give her the injection. The old woman brought water in a big vessel and replied, 'She is my granddaughter, born to my daughter. Orphaned as a child, I brought her up; now, she is all that I have and I live on her meagre earnings. How could she think of doing this to me?' the old lady started sobbing again.

Deeply touched as he was, Raghavan said nothing as he washed his hands. As he prepared to leave, he handed the old woman some pills and said, 'Don't worry. She'll wake up in a short while. Then give her some buttermilk, or even plain water; nothing else. Give her one of those tablets every two hours.'

'What about soda?' the old woman trotted behind him, as he stepped outside the hut.

'Oh, yes. Come and report to me in the morning. I'll prescribe accordingly.' He turned once more to take a long look at the young woman, and then left. Behind his back, he heard the old woman bless him heartily.

It was not long before the young woman herself came to see him at his clinic. Raghavan had no trouble finding out what she did for a living, and her problem after all, though she had her head down and had remained silent for most of his enquiries.

As he thought about her and the old woman, he realized that their inherently weak dispositions rendered them sort of handicapped in taking on life's struggles in an upright manner, twisting their fates, leading them to their present doom. He also wondered what drove her to her rash decision, which might have left her poor grandmother all alone, as the latter herself lamented on that fateful day.

'She is all I have, and I live upon her meagre earnings. How could she do this to me?'

The young woman had conducted herself with utmost dignity. As she rose to leave after the consultation, she had laid two rupee notes on the table. Tears welled up in her eyes and her diffident posture conveyed what she did not express in words: 'This is all I can give you in gratitude for saving my life.'

Raghavan said, with an anguished smile, 'Of course, this is my profession, but I don't take money from everyone.' Biting her lips, she meekly took back the notes; Raghavan asked her to be seated. Looking at her intently, he asked her, 'What you do for a living, may I ask?'

She realized that he had mistaken her for a sex-worker; she calmly replied, 'Nothing of disrepute, sir. However, placing my trust in a disreputable person has brought me shame and sorrow,' she faltered, remembering what still haunted her senses, though it had left her womb.

Raghavan had no inhibitions though, and he blurted out, 'Do you mean your miscarriage?'

She trembled at those words, and unable to meet his eyes, she hung her head again. With tears streaming down, she replied, 'I never meant to abort it; I only wanted to take my own life. I had no wish to live after committing such a crime either.'

Raghavan interrupted her sobs. 'I am aware of all that. I was only trying to get to know you and what you do for a living. If you are constantly feeling guilty about something, you are bound to take offence at every little thing. Your biggest crime was your suicide attempt. Had you a little more faith in your man and given him courage, you could have been better off.'

She cut him through vehemently, 'Ah, can courage be given? And what use is it to cowards anyway?' Raghavan could see that she was seething with fury at the bloody coward that had deserted her.

He waited for a few moments to let her simmer down and resumed conversationally, 'By the way, you haven't yet answered my question. I am just wondering what job you have, a single woman, not that educated and all, hmm?'

She calmed herself and began with a prelude, 'I shall tell you, but please don't presume that my fate has anything to do with my profession. I am an actress.'

'In the movies?' asked Raghavan who was not much into it anyway.

She replied with a dry smile, 'No, at the theatre. Of course, I had dreams of becoming a film actress, but not anymore.'

That was all he needed to know about her. In her subsequent visits, he remained professional, treating her health and gave her no advice or counsel; he did not believe in such things. In the couple of years that followed, he had forgotten about her, quite naturally.

But this day, as he saw her in a much sorrier state than ever before, he remembered all that he had known about her. She had grown 20 years older in the past couple of years. He asked her kindly, 'What happened? I can see that the loss of your grandmother has taken a toll on you.'

She just sat there tongue-tied, and head down. Raghavan waited for several moments but in vain. So finally he asked, feeling truly concerned, 'What brings you to me, at this hour?'

'I have come to you, because now I don't want to take my own life.'

Now he turned silent. She went on, 'I cannot afford to go to a gynaecologist, you see.' He looked up at her at these words. He realized that she had completely transformed.

She could perceive his unsaid words, 'Is this you who's talking? You who'd rather die?'

'Then I had my reputation to care for. Now I have no such qualms. That I am fallen is no secret.' She sighed, recalling her past display of pride and dignity before this very man.

'What you are proposing is lawfully a crime, and humanitarianly a sin. What happened in the past could be seen as an accident resulting from your suicide attempt, but now, it would be despicable and an utterly selfish act. Please change your mind.'

'Oh, this man is so pedantic,' she thought.

'If abortion is a sin, then what of an illegitimate conception? Isn't it kinder to let it die rather than letting it live a life of a bastard? This sin is nothing compared to what I would earn if I am cursed all my life for being such a mother; for even as a consolation, whom can I point to as the father, or even think of one?' She spoke intermittently, gathering her diverse thoughts, flexing and fidgeting with her fingers all the time.

Raghavan thought about her words and the horrendous feelings that evoked them; after some careful thought, he realized she was right, and it stunned him.

For a long time, they talked over it, like two like-minded friends.

Finally, he invited her to have dinner with him. In the meantime that roughly filled an hour, he deeply reflected on whatever passed between them, and said something with utmost determination—that which terrified her and made her doubt that either of them must have gone mad!

He said, 'It's a crime to kill. To abort the child is a shame to my profession and your femininity. If all you need is a father for the child, by all means, take my name. Dr Raghavan shall be your child's dad. I shall not deny it in the name of anything. I swear.' His words were laced with utmost passion and left her spellbound.

A momentary gaze passed between the two. Raghavan realized that the drama accompanied his words had robbed them of its credibility; so he continued in a matter-of-fact tone. 'Don't think I am taking pity on you. There is something of self-interest as well. You see, my claiming to be the father of your child shall naturally evoke a scandal about our supposed affair. It will be the talk of the town, and I would so welcome that...' Raghavan stared into space, as though picturing those happenings.

Radha was moved at the thought that he had been so much in love with her, of which she had been unaware and unworthy! Oh, how she had wasted herself! She threw herself at his feet and wept, 'Oh you are my saviour! I shall spend all my life at your feet! I shall bear any number of children for such a man!'

Every single word of hers, half-blurted out, half-whispered, pierced his heart like sharp needles, and gave him immense pain; the pain spread across his face, as though physical, as he broke down and wept like a child.

Radha was dumbstruck at this unexpected outburst of a grown male's voice in a loud tremor. He kept his back to her until his heavy sobs subsided; calming himself slowly, he turned to face her.

'Radha, pardon me if I have awakened any futile desires. I can be father to only this child that you are carrying. You see, I am not what you think...' and he drew near her ears to let her in his much guarded secret.

Yes, that was something he could not bring himself to talk candidly, as was his usual way. For once, he felt so personal about sex and very deeply at that.

As Radha heard what he had to say, she hugged him and shook her head violently, 'No, it cannot be! It's not true!' She thought of all those cowards who came to her in the dark and vanished at daybreak. And here was a man, who had cleansed her soul and given her a new lease of life. Radha had no doubt who was the most virile of them all.

Cupping his face with both hands, Radha sensed in his visage a gallant radiance such that she had never before witnessed in any man. Embracing him ecstatically, she felt her heart brimming with pride and joy. A steady flow of tears kept trickling from Raghavan's gently shut eyes onto her earlobes.

THE PALLBEARERS

Like Death's very own messenger, the policeman went knocking on every door in that colony. He could not deem this enquiry as one of his mundane tasks. Dreading the imminent doom, heart quivering, he looked up at the lady of every house and asked the same question: 'Amma! Is there a boy in your house, about 10, wearing khaki trousers and a white shirt?' he stammered.

The woman was hanging out her laundry. The policemen's eyes welled up with tears, as he watched her engrossed in her simple chore. She looked back at him, 'Why, yes, what's the matter?' and then she called out, 'Hey you, come here.' A boy came trotting from outside the house, only to take cover behind the folds of his mother's saree, in fright, upon seeing the cop.

'Oh, never fear, dear,' his mother cajoled him. 'He's harmless. Come and show yourself.'

The constable sighed. 'No Amma. That's not necessary. There, beside the flyover, a boy got hit by a truck...his head got mashed and...' words failing him, the good man shuddered, cursing his eyes that had sinned by witnessing the disaster.

'Oh my God! Is the child alive?' The policeman sighed again heavily and trotted towards the next door. 'I was told that the boy lived in this colony. Please take good care of your children, Amma.'

At the next door he stood and began. 'Amma, is there a boy in your house...?'

A woman stepped out saying, 'Oh, we haven't got any kids!'

'Ah, you blessed soul!' cried out the constable, clearly relieved and proceeded to discover that unfortunate woman who had lost her cherished treasure and probably didn't know it yet.

As he faced each woman in the colony, he hoped and prayed she was not the cursed one; but he knew the ominous truth; someone here was destined to be, and he wanted to flee immediately, never to look back. He could not imagine the dreadful tragedy unfolding in front of his eyes any moment.

In utter despair, he sat down on the porch of a house; his mouth was dry and sweat trickled down his exhausted spine. Taking his cap off, he wiped his sweaty brow and face with his hanky.

He badly wanted to give up the dreaded task and leave the place for good.

But how would that solve anything? the policeman thought to himself. After all, the child must have a mother. Oh boy, if only the child had none, it would be of some cheap comfort. How could a mother be deprived of her child that she so lovingly bore within her womb? What right has God to let that happen? Oh no, God is the benevolent creator. It's Yama, God of Death, who's cruel enough for such things; but then God created Yama too. Why does he allow Yama such mischief? If only God himself bore labour pains every time he created a new life, he wouldn't take one away so easily. The loss of a loved one's life is far more tragic than one's own. Oh my God!

Say, hasn't each of these women half a dozen kids to claim? Can't one cope with a single loss, fairly? Never! After all, if a childless bloke like me could be devastated thus, the plight of the boy's kith and kin, especially the mother's, is unspeakable.

It is one thing for a mother to lose a sick child that has suffered for long, before giving up; though that is tragic too; but to lose a hale and healthy one in a disastrous accident as this? Her one mammoth shriek could be agonizing enough to take her own life.

Oh bloody God, why do you have to create both birth and death? It was not a few moments ago that I saw the boy fluttering about like a little bird. He was holding an ice cream stick. I was just helpless and could do nothing when it all happened in a flash. It was fate that put me there tongue-tied, helpless, with my eyes open wide to bear witness. The boy hadn't even screamed. Death came too quickly for that; and it tugs at my heart that his little soul must have yearned for the uneaten ice cream he held. That's the worst thing about death; untimely and unexpected death is what leaves deadly devastation at its wake. With a fair notice, death shan't be so fearful. But then, it's not so kind. Almost all souls die with painful longings. Yes, no matter how much one lives, death is looked upon with dread. Wasted lives!

For instance, that day at the station, a little sparrow fluttered about within, chirping happily with its mate. The female bird kept teasing her love, and went and hid inside a recess in the wall. The male felt a gush of passion and angrily glared at his mate. The female did not budge. Oh, if only she had come back to him! The next moment, the male bird took off with a vehemence as the inspector and I shared furtive glances, expectant of the imminent romance…

I chuckled, hiding my own excitement and quipped, 'Oh, come on, sir, isn't it but natural for all that lives?'

No sooner did I utter those words, there was a loud shriek and the male fell dead at my feet. Its head was covered in blood. I looked up in horror, to find the ceiling fan above, rotating noisily.

The inspector hurried forward and picked the bird up in his hands. 'What a pity, old boy, did you mean death?' he added bitterly, as he threw the dead bird out of the window.

What was worse than the little chap's death, was the futile longing of his mate. Damn, God is a brutal murderer; more vicious than the most barbarous psychopath killer. How valid is the existence of love, affection, and pleasure, when death is close at hand, any moment?

'Could a child be allowed to die before he finishes eating his ice-cream? Oh merciless God! Yes, I ask you, for your sake! How can you allow such a death? What's your hurry, you bloody idiot? He had not even taken a single lick of the ice cream...it lay intact on the mud!' Thus, diverse thoughts clouding his mind, the constable sat for a long time on the porch, before he got up again sighing heavily.

He put his cap on and caught sight of a young mother nursing her baby, sitting by the window of her house. It was indeed a very tender sight to behold.

The policeman approached her and asked for some water to drink. With her baby still latched onto her breast, the woman fetched him a glass of water. The baby could be heard feeding hungrily from her mother, as the mother fondly stroked the baby's head with maternal delight.

The policeman felt a sense of foreboding. Could she be the mother? No, it could not be. She seems so young.

Anyway, 'Well, Amma! Is this your first child?' he began.

'No, this is my fourth. My eldest is a boy, and then I lost two children prematurely.'

'Where is your elder son now?'

'He's at school.'

'Which school? And what clothes were he wearing, please?'

'White shirt and khaki trousers; that's his uniform. Why do you ask?'

The policeman swallowed hard and asked in a casual tone, 'Is his school next to the flyover?'

'No, it's this way around. But he's very naughty; roams about all day and hardly obeys me. This morning he threw a huge tantrum for four *anna*s to buy ice cream. When I refused, he had gone and picked my purse. I barely caught him just as he rushed out. I had had enough of his pranks; I got so mad that I yelled after him, "Get lost, you little devil!"'

The policeman cut her short, 'Oh dear, you shouldn't have said that.' He lowered his head to hide his tears; after a short pause, he cleared his throat and with a determined air of a soldier at duty, he lifted his head. His tightly shut eyes failed to block the steady flow of tears that welled up; his heart now burst with the grave bitterness he had held for so long, and he stood in front of her stonily as he spoke 'There's a boy, like what you've just described, lying dead beside the flyover, Amma. Please go and check if he's yours.'

No sooner had he finished speaking, than the young mother let out a scream that echoed about the entire colony 'Oh God...my darling son!' The policeman dropped dead on the porch again, exhausted.

With the baby held on to her chest, she tore down the street, shrieking madly. Halfway through, she tucked the baby on her hips, the feeding breast now peeking from her unbuttoned blouse, but did she care? She was a mother, in dreadful panic!

The mob, deep in discussion about the gory details of the accident, now diverted its attention towards the woman coming running haphazardly. Now, the drama was about her, after all!

'What happened?' as one of them asked, with an air of mere curiosity. Another replied, 'A boy got hit by a truck…'

'And then?'

'Ha ha! What else? Massive roadkill indeed,' he laughed hysterically.

'These truck drivers ought to be punished for rash driving,' piped in a sanctimonious third.

Their expressions were all more of amusement than anger.

The policeman now came running round the street corner. Fit enough to outrun a robber, but not a loving mother, he had trailed behind.

Reaching the spot in a mad run, the young mother stopped short, as she heard the wails and laments of another, rolling on the floor, crying her heart out. The woman lifted her voice up and sobbed loudly to the skies above. 'Oh God, are you blind?'

Tears flowing uncontrollably, the one who came running now laughed! 'This is not our dear one, darling…this is someone else!' And hugging her baby tightly to her bosom, she smiled again. Her chest was still heaving with pent-up agony. Slowly subsiding, she became self-conscious and covered her half-naked breast. Turning to the policeman who came and stood next to her, she babbled, 'No sir, it's not my son, not he!' and she looked above to offer a prayer to the heavens.

The policeman was disgusted beyond words '*Chee*! Is this all? Is this what the much glorified motherhood all about? Is it an emotion that's so selfishly confined?'

Then all of a sudden, he caught sight of the wailing woman who was the cynosure of all eyes; he was shocked. She was none other than his wife, possibly on her way home from the market; her basket cast aside and the vegetables strewn in the mud.

'Idiot woman, why should she suffer so?' he frowned testily; however, his own tears failing to subside, he now wept bitterly like a child.

'Thangam, what is the matter with you?' chiding her, he helped her up.

'Dear, did you see what has happened? How dreadful! Is there nobody to prevent such a catastrophe? What about the police, what about our laws? Why do they let this happen? We waited for 20 years in vain. And now here's a treasure strewn away in the mud!' she howled in pain.

'Thangam, are we to weep so for a stranger's sorrow? Please get up. You're crazy, my dear. Come, I'll take you home,' and he gently helped her on her feet. She freed herself from his arms and ran back to the spot. 'He's my child, yes he's mine!' she shrieked madly.

The policeman now saw her, the woman who was coming towards the scene, with an air of nothing more than curiosity, with a strange confidence that it could not be 'her loss'. He stared at that terribly unfortunate woman.

Oh dear! How great is her misfortune, for sure?

Not wanting the least to witness what was about to unfold, nor let his wife do so, he held her hands firmly, and ushered her away from the crowd. She kept lamenting all the way home, as she sauntered weakly beside her husband. 'I've been deprived having a child of my own. Am I not even allowed to mourn the loss of one?'

The mob split into two, one group choosing to follow the drama of this sorry old couple.

As the couple entered their house in the corner of the street, they heard the dreaded explosion. The policeman shut his ears tightly to keep off the harrowing cries that set the entire vicinity ablaze. His wife tried to run back, impulsive to partake in the mother's anguish. Her husband held her tightly and almost carried her into the house.

What she held in her heart was not her own personal sorrow, but that of every mother in this world, who had lost a child; she seemed poignantly heavier to her man, who deeply felt the pain just as much.

As soon as they were indoors, they embraced each other and wept bitterly. The policeman turned to see prying eyes by the windows and the open front door, and hurried to slam it shut.

The curtains being drawn on this drama, the mob ran back to the accident spot.

Of course, if you're one of the mob, you'll find the whole thing mere drama, nothing more!

THE GUILTY

Raman caught sight of the young man at the bus terminal who was fully packed and all set to leave town; he felt a malicious delight.

'Ah, mission accomplished!' thought Raman, an evil grin spreading across his face.

The youth stood gazing blankly into the space. He looked sad, shocked, and his eyes were wet with tears.

'Hmm, such rogues deserve no pity, whatsoever,' reassuring himself, Raman cleared his throat as he ventured to talk to the lad. 'Off to a long trip, are we?' his tone mildly affronting.

The lad turned around and gave him a puzzled look. 'Pardon me sir, but do I know you?'

Raman was taken aback. 'Don't you know me? Are you not a tenant of No. 17, Main Road?'

'Not any more, sir. It's true that I was,' the young man gulped.

'Why? Have you quit the place?'

'I have; not at my will, though. My landlord Mr Sundaralingam...Oh, but I mustn't say anything against him; I have only my own fate to blame!' he sighed. 'All of a sudden, this morning he came and asked me to leave right away; he was also very angry, if I may add.'

'Did you ask him why?'

'I might have, if I was paying him rent. After all, he was being charitable, taking pity on my poverty. I ought to be grateful for his kindness.'

'Didn't you pay any rent, then?'

'I am a penniless fellow, sir. An orphan by birth, I managed to pursue my education, only thanks to the various kind souls in my life. If I could just get through another year of teacher's training, I shall find a job and make my own living; stop being anybody's burden. That has been my life's biggest ambition. Because, you see, for the past 22 years, I have been living upon charity. How could I bear a grudge against those who have been generous to me, even if they mistreat me at some point? Oh no, it's my bloody fate, sir.' He flushed and choked as he fought hard to hold back tears.

Raman stood stunned.

'Well then, really, don't you recognize me?' he asked meekly.

'No sir, I wonder who you are, you being so kindly concerned and all?' The young man wiped his tears.

'I live in the house right opposite to Sundaralingam's,' Raman looked keenly into the young man's face, scrutinizing it for any trace of betrayal.

'Really? Please pardon my ignorance by far. Glad to make your acquaintance, sir,' the young man said smilingly.

His innocuous smile sliced through Raman's heart. 'I am a clerk at the Collector's office...Listen, why did Sundaralingam ask you to vacate?'

'I am not sure, sir; he said something about getting complaints; wonder who complains of me, and of what? How does it matter, anyway? I have no right to stay there, if it displeases him. So that's that.'

A silence fell for a few moments. Not completely, though. Raman's conscience was screaming within him.

'Oh! What have I done? What a mighty mistake, a great sin that I have done! I am nothing but a scoundrel. How could I have suspected this child, this innocent orphan of a youth? I have brought unjust shame in this man's life! *Chee chee*, I am no human!'

'Sir, are you standing here for my sake?'

'It's ok, young man. Listen, if you don't mind, you can come and stay in my house.'

'Yes, I mean it,' Raman added to himself.

'Oh, thank you very much, sir; but a friend of mine in Washermanpet has invited me to stay with him. Thankfully, there are enough such kind souls ready to help me. Sometimes, it's kind of depressing, you know? I yearn to become someone who could help others and not be a bitter burden. Truth be told, I haven't been a cause of annoyance to anyone ever, except Mr Sundaralingam. Well, it's my fate. Here comes my bus, so I take leave of you. You are very kind, sir. Thank you very much!'

Raman stood there in dismay long after the youth boarded the bus and left. His heart ached with his parting words, 'You are very kind, sir, thank you very much.'

Wrenched with agony, Raman held his weak chest and dropped down on a bench.

Janaki, Raman's second wife was not only strikingly pretty, but younger to him by a score of years. Now, how does that justify Raman in suspecting every young man in the neighbourhood? Raman was not a bad man, and generally good-humoured. It was not in his nature to be irrationally suspicious of his wife or anybody for that matter. However, he was gripped with a deep and baseless mistrust, when a young bachelor came to rent the front portion of the opposite house. As the saying goes, 'as the fool thinks, so the bell clinks', the more Raman suspected the boy, the more his fears were reinforced.

'...the rascal always sits by the window, book in hand — pretending to read all day with the lights turned on. However, all he ever does is peep at my house, like a voyeur. Oh look! The moment he catches my eye, he is hiding behind his book...the cunning scoundrel!' thus Raman nurtured hatred and wrath against the boy, day after day.

One day, Raman returned early from work and found the lad loitering in front of his house. 'Ah, when I am not around, he lets down his guard, does he? Wonder what mischief he has up his sleeve! There! The rascal has craftily pretended to look away. What now, star-gazing in mid-afternoon? Do I seem stupid, my boy? I have crossed your age and know all your funny ways, mind you!' he growled to himself.

Yes, that's the truth! Raman had been a real scoundrel in his youth, and hence he suspected the lad on similar terms. Today, however, he was not happy just gritting his teeth at the boy. He turned to his wife.

'Look at this woman! Setting her mirror upon the front window — Idiot! Is there no other place in this house for decking up? Oh bother, does she have to lift both hands like that coquettishly, to comb her hair for the umpteenth time?! There she goes humming a *keerthana*, an *alaap* at that, my foot!'

Raman was fretting and fuming with rage. 'This pretty little tableau seems to be a daily routine. Pity I disrupted it today, by my coming home early. Oh, just you wait and watch, both of you!'

'Hey, you are early today,' bubbled Janaki.

'You got a problem with that? Run along and get my coffee,' Raman barked at her and slammed the window shut.

'My goodness. I can't bear this torment any longer! I can't entertain such funny business! Before it's too late, I must do something. Oh, what's to be done now?' Raman thought hard and made a decision and lost no time in talking to Sundaralingam.

'Are you sure? He is a gem of a boy! Very innocent and childlike. Such wrong antics are beyond him, sir!' Sundaralingam was flabbergasted.

'Do children remain children forever? I don't blame him; after all he is young; however, we can't turn an indulgent eye in these matters, can we?'

'Oh, I never would have believed him to be of such impudence!'

'How are we to guess all this? Actually, I learnt this from my wife who's very upset. Poor young thing, she is so timid and scared, you know?'

'Alright, sir. You please rest assured. I'll teach that boy a lesson,' growled Sundaralingam. Obviously, the boy had to leave.

'You are very kind, sir. Thank you very much!'

Raman sat down and wept. 'Oh, what a bloody villain I am!' he continued to hold his throbbing chest as he traipsed back home.

Upon reaching his house, he heard Sundaralingam calling him, 'Sir...'

Raman couldn't face him; he was wracked with guilt.

'I've chased that rascal out; bloody loafer! Serves him right!' Sundaralingam shouted heartily.

Raman made no reply but hurried inside his house. He saw that the front window stood open whereas the boy's window and door were both firmly shut.

'Janaki…' he called out gently.

'Yes?'

'You know, the boy who lived in Sundaralingam's house? Heard that he has vacated this morning. That's why the window remains shut,' he began conversationally.

'What nonsense? You know of nothing but your clerical duties. There's no boy or baby there. That window always remains shut,' Janaki snapped at him, dismissively.

'Oh my God! Am I the only one who was guilty?!'

As Raman took off his shirt, he secretly wiped the now unstoppable flow of salty tears. The poor orphan's words kept ringing in his ears: 'You are very kind, sir. Thank you very much.'

It's Only Words

Dark as the night was, Rukmini sat at the front steps of the charity hall waiting, her sensitive ears keen and alert, as if they were expecting somebody's imminent footsteps.

The old and dilapidated hall stood on the outskirts of the village, at the bend of the trunk road leading to the highway. The banyan tree came alive with the hustle and bustle during the daytime. The railway station stood just across the road and passengers, wayfarers and hawkers thronged the small tea-shop for refreshments. As night fell, both the tea shop and the adjacent betel shop shifted their sales to the touring talkies tent at a furlong's distance, targeting the film-goers.

All day long, Rukmini sat under the banyan tree weaving baskets and mats, chattering gaily with Muniyammal, the *masal vada* seller. A bundle of palm leaves and bamboo sticks lay beside her. A small crowd always circled her, watching her work with awe.

No matter what she talked or with whom, her nimble fingers kept weaving the palm leaves incessantly. The carving knife that she deftly held was so sharp that the slightest slip could slice her fingers; however, she never once faltered. It was as though her fingers had eyes. And that's only where she had them, for she was congenitally blind.

Ten years ago, a man called Sengeni had brought Rukmini as a 10-year-old girl to this village and cared for her like his own daughter. He had said, 'Here Rukku, you are a blind child and you have nobody but me. And even if you had kith and kin, they could only grudge keeping you. After I'm gone, I don't want you to go begging for a living. Please try hard and learn this craft; it will keep you from starving, as long as you live.' And he had taught her little fingers the craft of weaving baskets.

Rukmini spent all her day working under the banyan tree and eating at the teashop. After the last shop was shut down and the noise died down, she retired for the night to the charity hall, all alone.

Darkness and loneliness were not strangers to Rukmini. When one is in pitch darkness, how does it matter if there is company or not? However, that man Kannappan who was there last week, and had been jovial company to talk to, had left for good. Rukmini found the lonely darkness hateful since then, if not fearful.

Tonight, having gone to bed earlier than usual, she was fully awakened by a strange dream. Yes, for those who wonder, the blind can dream! When they can sleep and wake up like the rest of us, there's no reason they can't have dreams as well! However, their dreams are filled with sounds of all kinds, varied voices and sensory feelings. She sometimes dreamt of her late godfather, the old man Sengeni talking to her affectionately, stroking her head. Tonight, however she had had the most unusual dream.

A gentle flute melody came wafting from a distance; now a little feeble, now more audible, a play of sounds. Suddenly it stopped and she heard someone singing, '*Gnanakkan onRu irundhidum bothile…*' (When you have the eyes of wisdom…)

The voice was unmistakable. 'Yes, Kannappa…it's you. Have you come finally? So, you have made the flute. I was so worried. I wondered if you were going to come back at all. Maybe you thought you were better off without being burdened by this blind girl. I am so glad you've come!' Rukmini exclaimed with delight, feeling every inch of his head, face, shoulders and chest with her eager hands.

'Blind? Who's blind?' He asked and began singing again, cupping her face in his palms.

'Even Brindavan is not far, for in your eyes I see the lord,' Kannappan's melodious voice filled the air and went straight through her heart.

'Where? Where? Kannappaa… tell me?' Rukmini was startled awake; there was no one around. Only the band was heard playing from the touring talkies.

'It's not yet time; the show is yet to begin…' Will Kannappan come at all, at least today? She sat up musing and longing, unable to go back to sleep.

The last passenger train usually arrived at 10 pm at the Arasangudi station and halted for less than two minutes. As it departed, it carried with it the remnant of lights in the station, leaving behind pitch darkness, at which owls began hooting from their hide-holes in the banyan tree, foxes howled from the graveyard, trucks sped away honking loudly on the highway, the old charity hall shaking with tremors. At the same time, the band began playing at the touring talkies, indicating show time.

A week ago, quelling the nightly sounds into naught, a heavy downpour raged for over an hour. As it slowly subsided, Rukmini sat huddled in the folds of her pallu, enjoying the serene sounds made by raindrops falling from the cracks in the ceiling and the bushes that grew along the porch, splashing onto the little pools on the muddy floor. A stray dog came running for shelter and cuddled fondly at her feet; she picked up her stick and shooed it away. It was just then…

He arrived.

Drenched to the skin, with no clue of his whereabouts in the darkness, wary of hitting anything or falling over, he trotted with his arms extended in the dark.

Hearing Rukmini shooing away the dog, he spoke to her. 'Is anyone there, Amma. Is this the charity hall I was told about?' He crawled up the steps into the hall.

'Yes, this is it. Where are you from?' asked Rukmini.

'I am from Vizhuppuram. What of a place, it's all the same to me. I travelled without a ticket and was thrown out. This would be my hometown now. A good Samaritan at the station told me about this place. I suppose I might spend the night here?' He took off his shirt, wrung it out and started wiping his hair dry.

'Why of course, yes. Stay as long as you like. Who's bothered?' Rukmini replied nonchalantly. Rolling a leaf of tobacco and chewing it, she sat huddled in a corner.

Leaning against a pillar, he fished out a beedi and struck a match to light it.

The dim light that switched from the match to the beedi, glanced for a second at both of them, who were not up to looking at each other, before dying into the darkness.

As though he lived just on smoke, he sat swallowing mouthfuls of it, suddenly feeling warm and cozy. After the third puff, the beedi's wrapper caught fire and smelled of soot. He quenched it at once and saved it for later. Tapping on the matchbox, he began singing merrily.

'When you have an eye of wisdom…' His voice resonated through the silent night. Rukmini sat up and listened. She liked both the song and his voice very much.

He was singing heartily. Once he finished, he cleared his throat; and only then did Rukmini return to her senses. 'Hey! You sing really well. It was quite good. Will you sing another song, please?' She drew herself closer to him.

Her praise, the way she did it, her voice that faltered and gave away her interest, gave him newly found vigour and pride.

'Another song? Hmm, can you give me some water to drink? Do you have some?'

'You'll find it in that corner. Help yourself, will you? By the way, what is your caste?'

'Padayachi, Amma. Where is this water pot, now?' He felt the floor with his hands.

'Wait, I'm coming,' she got up and walked easily up to the accustomed corner and handed him a tin mug of water. 'Here you are…and I am Padayachi too.'

He stretched out his hands towards her, as she called out. As he took the mug from her hands, his fingers brushed against hers.

'Hmm…what is in a caste, after all,' he murmured.

'Well, why did you travel without a ticket? And where are you headed to?' asked Rukmini.

'This has been my routine for the past four years. I sing on the train for money. Some days I get even a whole buck. Always, north of Vizhuppuram, I don't come down south. And most of the officers know me, and don't mind. Today there was someone new, and he showed me out.'

'Don't you have a home, wife and kids of your own?'

He did not reply to that but laughed rather loudly. It was a dry and bitter laugh. So Rukmini wondered if he was too young for all that and she had made a faux pas! At this thought, she couldn't help laughing as well. 'How old are you?' she asked him amidst the mirth.

'Oh, I am as old as a mad horse.'

'I asked your age…not the mad horse's!'

'What matters, how old I am? I am 22. With my mother gone, I was orphaned in my own house. My stepmother was cruel and my father negligent; they had other kids. With nobody and nothing to call my own, I finally quit. It's been four years now. Fate brought me hither tonight; goodness knows where, tomorrow. I have no kith or kin, or home of my own. You see, in the whole wide, wide world, we are each alone, yet we are all together, aren't we?' he sighed.

'Did you have anything to eat?'

'No. I have two *anna*s. But where am I to go and buy food here in this wilderness?'

'Here, eat some peanuts. Eat them and sing me another song. You sing very well.' She untied a cloth pouch, took a handful of peanuts and held it out to him. He held her hand in the darkness, and shifted the peanuts to his palm, careful not to spill them.

'Ok, what do you want me to sing…?'

'Anything…'

'*Unnazhagai kaana iru kangal poadhaathe…*' (To behold your beauty, I need but more than a pair of eyes…) he tapped the match box and kept rhythm.

As Rukmini was lost in the melody, the dog sneaked up to her again, seeking shelter at her feet. Irritated, she picked up the stick and aimed a hit that did not miss its target. The dog ran away howling in pain.

'What's that? Is that a bamboo stick? Show it to me...' he held out his hand in the darkness.

'Yes, why do you ask?' Rukmini handed it to him.

'It's a nice bamboo...' he stroked the stick.

'It's a nice bamboo, for making what?'

He laughed gently.

'Why do you laugh?'

'Nothing, a nice bamboo is of many uses; in the hands of the blind though, it comes to naught.'

Rukmini felt a tug at heart, thinking he meant her. 'You wait and see, I'll show you what all I can make out of it.'

'What can you make, pray tell me.'

'Baskets, mats, coasters...'

'Really? I can make a flute out of it, you know?'

'A flute...? Really? Do you know how to make it, play it?' Rukmini asked him eagerly.

'Well, all these songs that I sang now, I can play on the flute just as well.'

'Very well, give me that stick. I'll find you a really nice one. Do make a flute and play it for me. Ok? Why are you not eating the peanuts? Here, take this stick.' She looked for a good bamboo stick from her pile and handed it to him.

He fell silent, blessing this good angel in his heart, who in the middle of a lonely night had given him food to eat and a stick to hold as well.

After a few moments of silence, she asked him, 'What is your name?'

'Kannappan, and yours?'

'Rukmini.'

'Hey Rukmini, are you not a woman of youth? Why are you alone in this charity hall, with nobody for company?'

'This has been my home since I was a child. I know no other place in this world. My only family, my grandfather died four years ago.' Rukmini was overwhelmed with thoughts of the fond old man and started crying. After heaving a couple of sobs, her grief died down somewhat.

'Hmm, so even if you are married off, this shall still be your maternal home. Am I right?' Kannappan broached the subject of marriage only to confirm her age that he had guessed by her voice.

'You are a man; I am a woman, and that too a blind one. I have nobody in this world; and even if I had, I might be no more than a burden to him. Therefore I am by myself, an orphan.'

Kannappan was shocked, as though a bolt of lightning struck him from top to toe. He said no more. Rukmini tried with all her might to continue the conversation, but he never replied. Believing he had fallen asleep, she too tried to go to sleep.

However, for long after this conversation, both of them remained quietly awake into the night.

The next morning as soon as she woke up, Rukmini called out, 'Kannappa! Kannappa!' No answer!

She felt the place where he had slept, with her hands. He was not to be found. She felt angry and distraught that he had left without even saying goodbye. For a while, she remembered the old man and lamented loudly. As the crowd around the banyan tree bustled as usual, she got up and went over to the teashop. After a cup of tea, she started painting the bamboo toys she had crafted the previous day.

She, who had never known anything about colours, painted the toys beautifully in different colours. She was slightly more informed about the colours, than the toys themselves were — for she knew that the green colour was always in the glass flask; blue colour, she kept in the tin mug; red was held within the coconut shell. That was all!

She painted with no definite pattern, but according to the whims of her heart. The Gods with eyes looked at them and praised their beauty!

On that day — when Kannappan had left without a word — Rukmini was unable to put her mind to work. She was not even up to chatting with her companion Muniyammal. She sat quietly, humming to herself, 'To behold your beauty, I need more than a pair of eyes...'. Muniyammal heard it and teased Rukmini. Rukmini laughed along with her. Yes, Rukmini was neither coy nor demure. She spent the whole day thinking about him.

And many days after that night, she was still thinking of him day and night. She imagined his voice and singing and found solace in it. She could not think of anything more wonderful than being with him, and listening to him sing, as long as she lived.

But that Kannappan, he was nowhere to be found!

She believed he would come back some day. And it was for him, she sat waiting.

As she sat there in the dark, chewing tobacco, after being awakened by dreams of him, the movie had begun in the talkies. The noisy band of the talkies and the teashop's creaky gramophone that was actually humiliating the old classical singers it played, had all died down.

In the silence of the night, there came a distant melody from a flute.

'It's the same song! Could it be Kannappan?' Rukmini trembled with delight.

The faint melody sounded louder as it drew closer. It suddenly stopped and she could hear clear taps of a bamboo stick close to her. As she heard footsteps on the front steps of the charity hall, 'Who's that? Is that Kannappan?' she asked.

'Yes…'

'Where have you been all along? I was so upset that you did not even say good bye.' As she said these words, he choked with tears and happiness. Unable to say a word, he sat down quietly.

'Where were you? Did you eat anything? I have rice soaked in water. Do you want to eat?'

'No Rukmini. I just ate. You so kindly gave me peanuts that day. Look, I got something for you today.' He handed her a packet of snacks.

'Have you found a job of sorts? Very well then. A youth like you must not beg for alms. What job, and where?'

'Just like you, I have begun a craft too.'

'What craft?'

'Well, remember that bamboo stick you gave me? I made a flute out of that; I sold it for eight *anna*s. Then I bought some more bamboo for two *anna*s and made flutes and whistles for little kids, and made a rupee out of them. Then I got myself a penknife, nails and stuff. Now I am well-versed in making flutes. You were my inspiration.' As he went on talking, Rukmini wanted to embrace him with joy. She eagerly drew herself closer and closer to him.

'Hey! Listen to me. Hmm, you know, I like you, your song, and everything very much. And…so, you and I, er…'

Yes, she was completely unabashed like a child. She who had never seen this world and its people with her naked eyes, was naturally unaware of their affectations and fake expressions. What she felt in her heart, she was letting out with her words.

Kannappan made no reply, but lit a beedi.

'Kannappa? Why are you silent? Please say something, or even better sing something. I was longing to hear you talk and sing, for a whole week, you know? By the way Kannappa? Have you seen any movies?' She tried to get him to talk.

'Oh yes, but that was long ago.'

'And now?'

'Where do I go for money for the tickets?'

'I'll buy the tickets. Shall we go? I'll sit listening, you watch the movie.'

'Ticket's fine. How am I supposed to watch without eyes? Rukmini, I am blind too. Four years ago, I got smallpox and lost my eyes. You are so affectionate, but what an unlucky cad I am, I can't even see your face! Until you said you were blind, I had the same wish as yours; but how can we live together? We won't be able to help each other. That's why I left without a word. But I did not have the heart to leave for good, without bidding you goodbye. I'll be leaving this town tomorrow morning. If only I had eyes, I'd never leave you. But what could be done. I must go. Please forget me!' Kannappan wept.

Rukmini was filled with sympathy for him. 'Hey, why do you cry for this? So what if we don't have eyes? I don't find anything amiss; you see, I have never realized what I lack, for I've never had them. I know I am blind because people say I am; that's all. Am I not happy? So it's no big deal to me that you're blind as well. Why should I let you go for something as trivial as that?'

'And, you say you once had eyes; you should tell me all about it! What are eyes Kannappan? what is this "seeing" that everybody talks about?' She touched his shoulder and eagerly drew close to his face. Kanappan felt a thrill run down his spine.

'Rukku? You know something? Eyes are nothing but YOU. Yes, you are the apple of my eyes, my dear.' Filled with ecstasy, Kannappan struggled for words.

Rukmini held out her hands and stroked his face, his head, his chest and shoulders with glee.

Inside that dark building, with not a soul to interfere, they began their tryst, talking all night about their lives and their love and longing for each other.

Beyond Cognizance

Success is an abstract thing in life. If fulfilment of expectations can be deemed success, then an expected failure is logically a success; not long ago, I was thus highly successful.

I had been to the town on a business, which, if successful, could be life-changing. As usual, I expected to fail, but lo and behold! I failed in my expectations and actually succeeded in my venture.

My failure could be described thus: Imagine you were yearning for the most beautiful damsel ever, but seriously lacked courage to open up to her, that even the very idea seemed ludicrous. However, one day you muster courage, (or recklessness) and make a proposal to her, only expecting to be mercilessly ridiculed! Well, imagine if the diva trashed all your fears and fell into your arms with absolute surrender, as though waiting for you all her life, oh! What a mighty failure it would be!

❈

I had to celebrate such a failure, or stupendous success, whatever! I couldn't wait until I was back home. It had to be that very moment; yes, I am that impulsive.

But then, celebration is abstract too. True celebration is the euphoria of the heart and has little to do with its expressions in real life — whether you choose to party or give away to charity!

Presently, I had a single silver coin in my pocket. A whole rupee! So what? It would do nicely for some celebration. But wait, there was a glitch. I needed three-fourth of it for my bus fare back home. I still had a quarter rupee left, didn't I?

A cup of freshly brewed coffee with a dash of creamy milk, with just a hint of sugar cost just two annas, but did me a lot of good! I felt instantly invigorated! Setting aside the 12 annas for my bus fare, I had just two annas left. Wondering what to do with it, I remembered the adage, 'Spend until the last penny like a king.'

Just then I heard a voice 'Oh, kind lord, please have mercy on a poor blind beggar.' He was sitting on a corner of the crowded platform of the railway station. In front of him lay an aluminium bowl. Amongst the few copper coins that lay within, now glittered the new two anna coin that I had dropped.

The beggar felt for the coin and folded his hands towards the direction he assumed I stood, and blessed me heartily; something that greatly gratified me, convincing me that my celebration was worthwhile after all!

I went to the ticket counter and asked for a ticket to my hometown. However instead of the ticket, the coins were handed straight back on my extended palm. 'Please give one more anna, sir.'

'But it's only 12 annas, right?'

'Oh, the tariff is revised starting today.'

I felt I had sunk inside a deep pit. Now, where am I to go beg for the single anna that I badly need?

There sits an old gentleman reading his newspaper. Why not I ask him…my idea was quelled as soon as it sprouted. The old man was not so gentle in refusing alms to another man who had likewise sought his generosity.

I reflected on the irony of life; within moments, I had turned from a noble benefactor to a lowly beggar!

'There, the shiny silver coin glittering inside the beggar's bowl amidst all the cheap copper coins is mine!'

'Are you sure? How can it be yours when you have already given it away, and received his gratitude as well?' my conscience replied.

'But now I am stranded! Am I not entitled to at least half of it? Yes, it lies within his bowl now, but wasn't it mine to start with? Suppose I ask him to return it? Oh no, and anyway how could he recognize me?'

'Perhaps I take it back myself? Well, there goes a fellow, dropping an anna, and picking up half an anna from the bowl; suppose I drop an anna and pick up my two anna coin?'

'That's cheating!'

'Cheating? No, I would have still donated him an anna. And I shall be contented with as much charity as of now; Yes, I am going to get back my anna.' Though I had reasoned well enough to myself, my hands trembled as I dropped an anna, picked up the two anna coin and stepped back.

'You rogue!' shouted the beggar. I startled and turned around. His blind eyes livid with shock, he asked me, 'Good lord, is this fair? You are taking away what a noble soul had generously given me, and giving me half of it back. Don't you dare cheat a blind man; you will rot in hell!'

Stung as though by fire, I dropped the two annas back in his bowl. Now I have given away three annas!

'Sorry... by mistake,' I stammered as my trembling voice almost gave me away.

A lady had dropped half-anna and taken a quarter-anna coin away. The beggar had immediately felt for his bowl to see if his precious two anna coin was still there. That's how I'd been caught. How could he bear to part with his rare treasure?

I stopped and reflected.

'Is it his money?'

'Yes, of course!'

'But I gave it to him!'

'Well, money can be lent; charity never!'

Thus, I stood for a long time, arguing with myself. My train arrived and left. The next train was due in a few hours. I enjoyed the fruit of my charity by walking all the way to the next station.

Remember that horrendous train accident in Tamil Nadu, two years ago? It was in all the papers. Well, that was the train I had missed.

Do you reckon it was my charity that saved my neck? Well, I don't know! It's beyond my cognizance.

❋ ❋ ❋

New Horizons

The little black cat scurried restlessly up and down the stairway, unable to find her dear mistress Indu anywhere about the house.

Dusk had set in and it was time to put on the lights; Indu's mother Kunjammal however, sat transfixed in one dark corner of the living room, as though both anticipating and hiding from someone she deeply feared.

The black kitten's eyes glittered in the dark and heightened her fears. The agitated kitty kept mewing, calling out for her mistress, as it climbed down the staircase.

Kunjammal shut her ears. The kitty's eyes seemed like her husband's. She thought about his imminent arrival and shuddered thinking of the events that would unfold thereafter.

The kitten now lurked beside her feet, mewing sadly. Kunjammal picked it up fondly, held it to her face and began to weep. The cat was surprised at this sudden display of affection from someone who always shooed her away; the shock calmed her down.

Kunjammal wondered if she could likewise calm the rest of the household when they learnt what had happened.

The cat wriggled out of her clutches and ran to the backyard, still mewing forlornly. Kunjammal's heart went out to the poor little beast.

For the cat was the sole companion of her daughter Indu, who had been banished to reclusion for the past four years within the confines of her room. Initially, when the magnitude of her 'crime' had not fully dawned upon her, Indu had spent all her time singing to herself and playing with the little kitten. Soon, fun and frolic subsided and she turned to intensive reading. Her younger sister Vijaya helped her by bringing her loads of books from the library. Recently, Indu had lost interest in pretty much everything and was often lost in deep thought, sometimes the silence breaking into huge sighs. The kitty was her only solace during those hours. Indu was likewise very fond of the cat, taking good care of her. How could she bear to leave her pet behind? Oh, how she sobbed while taking leave? Had her love for her pet partaken in her tears? However, she had clearly put her foot down – 'I am not ready to sacrifice my life for anybody in this world.'

'Leave alone, what she had said. How did I manage to let her go?' Kunjammal marvelled at her own bravado.

Of course, I was right to do that; but can one always pull off all right deeds without fear? She pondered over those moments of enormous courage and felt thankful. Even as she trembled with fear at the consequences, she had no doubt that she had done right; nevertheless, she also realized that she wouldn't be as strong, if the moment were to repeat itself.

She also realized that, it was a momentary impulse that drove Indu to elope with him at 17. Sometimes, impulsive actions that seem irrational are albeit based on strong reasoning. And even when the moment of impulse dies down, its rational aspect stays intact.

The mother went on reflecting deeply; 'It's only after four long years, now, that I am able to empathize with her actions. Is it possible that the others would as well?' She felt a dread of apprehension.

By then, the cat again loomed in front of her, with questioning eyes: 'Where is Indu? Where is Indu?'

Soon, the rest of the household would come pelting her with questions; what should she tell them?

Though she was the lady of the household lording it over its members, she felt guilty of a breach of authority.

Except for Indu, who had again eloped, this time with her blessings, the rest of the family will soon be here and she dreaded facing each of them—her mother-in-law who has gone to the temple; Ambi, her son who was at school; Vijaya, her younger daughter, who'd come home dallying around long after college hours; and finally, her husband who was probably then playing bridge at the club. She wondered who she would be facing first, and how.

Kunjammal's face was covered in sweat. The house was now pitch dark and the lights were not yet on.

Grandma came home first. As the temple's yard was swampy and sludgy with the recent rains, the usual *upanyaas* had been cancelled and she had to return home early; else she'd be the last.

As soon as she opened the gates and walked in, she could be heard saying, 'Why is the house so dark? Is there a power failure? Where is Indu? Indu! Indu! Why haven't you called the electricity board?' Groping in the dark, she set out towards Indu's room adjoining the terrace, climbing the staircase, supporting her weak knees with one hand, and holding on to the railing with the other.

Grandma never tired of climbing up and down that staircase a hundred times a day. She was the tiniest of them all, and it was amusing to note that she was mother to the tall and hefty Ramabhadran. Ramabhadran hated the staircase. He was not up to climbing it up even once without panting, especially after hypertension and heart problems had set in;

his maximum driving speed came down to 15 kmph; so he was a perfect stranger to Indu's room; Kunjammal could not bear to set foot in her daughter's room who enraged her so much. Vijaya had her own room downstairs. It was only Ambi and granny who never minded climbing up and down to pay Indu a visit. Granny always called out her dear granddaughter's name as she climbed up, as though she believed that would alleviate the exertion.

Kunjammal, however, could not bear grandma addressing Indu in such dulcet tones. She abhorred the very name of her daughter. Four years ago, on that fateful day, when Indu was forcefully brought back from her elopement and imprisoned by her father, Kunjammal went upstairs to curse and spit on her daughter's face. 'Oh, why don't you kill yourself, you shameless whore?' That was the last she ever saw or spoke to her daughter, until today — two hours ago.

Perplexed that the neighborhood was lit with power, grandma felt for the light switch in Indu's room and the sight she saw! Shelves empty, things strewn across the floor, a clear sign of something out of the ordinary.

'Indu, hey Indu!' grandma shouted as she came running down again; seeing the tiny light from the kitchen, she called out, 'Kunjammal, where is everyone? Indu! Are you here?' and proceeded towards the kitchen.

An anguished voice from behind stopped her in her tracks. 'Indu's not here.'

Granny turned but could see nobody in the dark. Switching on the lights, she demanded, 'Pray tell me what do you mean by sitting here in this darkness?'

Kunjammal's lips quivered; she suppressed her sobs and looked up at her mother-in-law. She spoke nothing for a few moments, but looked up at the older woman with her eyes red with tears. Grandma stood in silence too, as though grasping things that were unsaid.

'Where is Indu?' She now questioned with a calmed down air.

'He was here; and she left with him.' Kunjammal replied hoarsely.

'Why on earth should the scoundrel come here? How could you let Indu go? Why didn't you send for her father at the club? He nabbed him once before, he would have hanged him this time for sure! She left with him, indeed...you crazy fool! Your husband will murder you for this.' Grandma wrung her hands in despair and collapsed on to a sofa nearby.

Kunjammal remained silent, having braced herself to face the worst until grandma completed her tirade. She then spoke slowly.

'Yes, we managed to punish him once; we managed to heap upon him every false accusation we could think of, forcing her to attest the same and jailed him. And then? What became of my daughter? Just think. Try as we might to gloss over the fact that they had lived together for about a month, who in the wide world believes that he had kidnapped her to steal her jewels. Even those greedy for our wealth, come asking only for Vijaya's hand. So what happens to Indu? Yes, your son would get him hanged, even kill him with his bare hands. What comes of it? Will Indu cease to be a problem for us? Can you deny that she's been one that we couldn't solve the past four years? Can we, at all? Give it a thought, mami!' As Kunjammal tearfully uttered each word weighing them with meticulous forethought, grandma became thoughtful too.

Heads down, now both of them sat in silence for several moments, only to suddenly look up at each other; at that very moment, Kunjammal no longer seemed as crazy or impulsive to grandma. However, she now shared her daughter-in-law's angst and fear about the imminent doom that was about to befall.

'How did it all come about? Why did you let her go? Oh, now what's to be done? Remember the last time he blamed both of us for everything; that it was all our fault, and that we used this office assistant Venu for domestic errands, invited him for suppers and made him part of the household. How could you forget that? And now he will accuse us again! Do you realize that?' Grandma shuddered as she clutched her daughter-in-law's shoulder for support.

Kunjammal held the fingers that touched her and sighed. She felt a bit courageous now. It could be explained only thus. As the saying goes one's fear makes another valiant, Kunjammal drew her courage from grandma's fear. In fact, she had only been dreading facing her husband before she could confide in somebody.

Kunjammal realized that grandma empathized with her and was coming to terms with Indu's predicament and their own helplessness in her regard. It had been just a few hours back that she stepped out of the kitchen to see Venu and Indu standing together on the verandah, looking straight up at her.

Her immediate reaction was fitful rage, at the sight of the youth who, in her eyes, had ruined her daughter's life.

There had been a heavy downpour and he was sitting on the wooden bench beside the bamboo blinds that hardly kept away the falling rain. Beside him, stood Indu with an air of utter submission, sobbing uncontrollably, her face covered with the end of her saree.

He spoke with tear-stricken eyes and lips that quivered with emotion: 'Indu, all these years that I spent in jail, I was wrought with guilt for having ruined an innocent girl's life, and saw my punishment was no more than my penance. Though, it broke my heart that they labelled me a "thief" and even led you to attest that, I could not bring myself to hate you, but only pity you so much. I felt my punishment was all the more justified for eloping with such an innocent child. But pray tell me now! Crazy and rash as it seems now, was it not true and mad love for each other that induced us to elope together, that fateful day? Yes, we did not realize that hunger and mundane worries soon follow love. Was it not you that had willingly handed me your jewels after my many futile but earnest attempts to secure us a living? Did I not vehemently refuse them until repeated coercion from you, insisting you were mine, body and soul; what of your jewels? Do you really believe our love was untrue? You are not a child anymore. Do you really believe I was after your jewellery? Please stop crying and do tell me!' As he implored her, reminding her of every painful detail from the past, Indu burst into sobs.

'Venu, please forgive me. I was a complete coward to have let you down, and put you behind bars. My mind was befuddled, and what once did not seem so wicked, now haunts me day and night, and I must pay my penance until I die.'

'Please don't cry, Indu. You've done nothing wrong. I am satisfied you believe I am innocent. No, don't cry please,' and he touched her shoulders in an attempt to quieten her.

At that sight, Kunjammal instantly felt her anger subside; not wishing to interrupt them, she stood in the hall, watching the poignant tableau.

She looked at Venu, her heart going out to him and his pitiful fate, all for falling in love with her daughter and thereby earning the wrath of her husband. Her eyes filled when she heard him console and forgive Indu, whose false witness had sealed his fate.

He could be heard saying, 'My imprisonment by law was for but four years; but then you were slowly getting imprisoned for life, by your own family. I could not get that thought out of my head, Indu. Yes, we were both guilty. But I have served my sentence and am a free man now. But you? I know not what I can do to salvage you, Indu.'

Now, Indu began speaking amidst broken sobs, 'Yes, we had both been guilty to have fallen in love, only because we did it then. My life was ruined because I eloped to get married, when I was not of age. Now, my life will remain ruined, if I do not. Therefore, if you were the one who wrecked my life, it's only you who can put it right. However, I dared not believe you could forgive me for what I had done to you, Venu,' Indu choked at her own words.

Kunjammal who had been listening to their conversation, behind the walls, covered her face and wept.

'Indu, are you serious? Are you thinking the way I am?' Venu questioned her, trembling with anxiety and joy.

Indu brushed away her tears, looked at him with reddened eyes and gave him a smile of consent and contentment.

He shut his eyes only to feel them brimming as well.

'Venu, take me along. Let me come with you. I have had enough of this hell. Mother heartily wishes I were dead, and hasn't kept it a secret from me. I too tried to take my own life, several times, but in vain. How I wish I could…' Indu wept fresh tears, recollecting some dark incident.

Indu continued, as Venu slowly gathered himself. 'However, thank goodness, I didn't do anything of that sort, Venu. You know, I never dreamt that you'd come back, however, subconsciously I had harboured such a hope, which had kept me alive, and for no other reason. Very well. I am coming with you, now. But we are not going to elope like before. We'll take everyone's leave openly. I am of age now, probably what I was waiting for within my prison upstairs. Yes, we'll bid our goodbyes and go.'

Venu watched her in awe and amazement, as she went on. He realized that this woman's face was not what he had beheld four years ago. This was the visage of a woman who had hit rock bottom in life, faced mortification, disappointment, and abuse of every kind, suffered in solitude and had been wrought anew by time. There was no trace of fallacy and her eyes glowed with a deep reflection of life and bright hopes for their future together.

He realized, 'This woman is no more a juvenile, plausible of being kidnapped. On the other hand, she is someone with whom one could join hands and face all the perils of the world.' He stood up gallantly, upon this newly found resolution.

It was then his eyes fell upon Kunjammal who stood by the hall stairway. He felt an upsurge of affection, remembering her motherly care towards him, once upon a time.

He greeted her respectfully.

Kunjammal felt her heart overflowing for him; however she hid her feelings and yelled at him, 'How dare you darken my doorstep? Get out at once!'

Indu turned to her, 'Mother, I am going with him too.'

'Oh, like hell you will! How brazen you are?' and she pushed her towards the staircase. 'Let us lock you up now. Venu, do you want me to call the police?'

Indu calmly replied, 'Mother, the law is not yours to misuse as you wish. You have no right to keep me locked against my wishes. Please call the police, and I shall speak to them.' Kunjammal was astonished at these words.

'Well, well, so things have come this far, haven't they? So much for bringing you up with love and care. This fellow means more to you than your own parents, eh?' groaned Kunjammal.

'Ah, love and care! Isn't that why father has imprisoned me here all these years? And isn't that why you have wished me dead, every single day since I returned? I have had enough being a slave to your whims. Let father come. I shall take his leave and be gone for good.' Indu replied fearlessly, her voice now louder.

Venu had stepped out of the house, and stood getting drenched in the rain.

Kunjammal's eyes traversed between both of them, for a moment.

She empathized with her daughter's vehemence. Of course, she's right. Her heart ached at the thought of secretly wishing her 'fallen' daughter dead, and praying to the Gods for the same.

Amidst a mother who wishes her dead, a father who has brutally imprisoned her for life, a family who shuns her with ridicule, there is but only this youth, who could give her a new lease of life.

She also realized that she was not honest with herself in yelling at Venu, and stopping them from getting together. And that realization was of immense magnitude.

'Very well, leave! Be gone this very moment! There is no need for you to take leave openly. If only you do, it will all surely come out in the open. No one is stopping you. Pray leave before anyone comes and does that,' Kunjammal wept imploringly now.

As it was now Indu and Venu's turn to look shocked, Kunjammal continued, 'I understand dear, you are right in wanting to join him. Just don't make a scene. Your father is not up to all this. Knowing him, I beg you not to engage in a duel with him; so leave immediately.'

The next moment, her daughter flung herself between her arms with heart-wrenching shrieks, 'Oh Amma!'

Oh! It had been ages since those two hearts experienced such an emotional exchange!

As they subsided, both felt a sense of urgency. Indu ran upstairs to get her things. Kunjammal sat down calmed, yet totally exhausted.

Moments later, Indu came back, suitcase in hand, all set to bid goodbye to her mother, who was sitting in a trance, eyes closed.

'Indu!' Kunjammal heartily embraced her daughter, who fell at her feet, seeking her blessings.

'Indu, my darling. Everything will be alright. May God be with you; Do write to me often. I will pray for you with all my heart, what else can I do? Forgive me Indu, for being a helpless mother,' cupping her daughter's face, her mother pleaded with her.

'Oh, Amma! How wrong I was to believe you hated me!' Indu sobbed in repentance.

Venu came towards them and looking at her suitcase, he said, 'Indu, there's no need for anything. I shall get you whatever you need. You must come as you are. And you must give up every single piece of jewellery that you are wearing, if you are to come with me.' Indu readily agreed, and went on to remove her earrings, nose ring, bangles, and necklace and handed them to her mother.

Kunjammal turned away as she could not stand her daughter's bare look, nor could she take the ornaments from her. Indu however, placed them beside her mother and called her 'mother' again.

Kunjammal turned to look at her daughter and said, 'Indu, do not forget! Please go to some temple and get a string like this tied onto your neck. This is the greatest piece of jewellery of them all, for women,' and she showed the wedding string around her neck.

'Yes, Amma,' and Indu again fell at her mother's feet; Venu joined her this time.

'Farewell, my children. My blessings to you for a good life. May God be with you!'

It stopped raining and dusk was setting in. The couple set out for a new life together. Indu felt a new vigour as soon as she stepped out of the house, and began walking briskly. As she turned around the street corner, she turned around to look at her mother's face one more time with tear-filled eyes. And then, she was gone!

Kunjammal traipsed back inside, to lay her eyes on the jewellery abandoned by her daughter and sighed heavily. Her next thought was, 'How could I let something like this happen?' stunned, she sat down on the stool.

Thankfully, grandma was home before anyone was, and she felt greatly relieved narrating the afternoon's incidents, as grandma could not hide her own sniffles and tears as she took them all in.

Grandma was indeed an ancient soul. Yet, her maternal instincts gave way to love and sympathy for her granddaughter, whose turmoil she had partaken in pain. After much pondering, she took sides with Kunjammal, ranting away her thoughts. Yet, she wept out of dread and anguish, blaming fate for having befallen thus. She even tried to console herself vehemently that it was good riddance of Indu who had brought nothing but dishonour upon the family. However, she felt a sense of foreboding, as she remembered her son's raging temper.

Just then a scooter could be heard on the streets. Kunjammal stopped her rant to observe, 'That must be Vijaya; wonder what takes her so long to be back from college?' she added tersely. The clock struck eight.

Grandma turned around to see nobody. 'Where is she, by the way?'

'Oh, hasn't he just dropped her at the street corner? She'll be here presently,' replied Kunjammal.

'Who?' blinked grandma.

'How do I know? You must ask her. She thinks I am blind to her funny ways. Goodness knows what troubles she has in store for us. The only reason she hasn't eloped with anybody is Indu, who preceded her. So much for a strict disciplinarian of a father! May be, it's all to do with my bad fate, oh God!' and she slapped her forehead, as Vijaya entered the house.

The two elder women sighed in despair, as Vijaya hurried towards her room, without a word.

Soon, Ambi was home too.

Meanwhile, Vijaya who had gathered the events of the day from the hushed-up talks, demanded of her mother, 'Oh Amma! What have you got to tell father? Hasn't she got you into a soup?'

'Oh! Look who's talking? Father's timid daughter, aren't you?' glared her mother.

'What have I done, now?' Vijaya retorted and tried to hid behind her grandmother.

'Thankfully nothing as yet, dear. Let things stay that way; will you?' replied her grandma.

After a moment's silence, Vijaya found her eyes welling up as she asked, 'Amma, will Indu never come back now? Won't I ever see her again? Oh Indu, what a beast I've been to you? I have insulted and ill-treated you many a time!' and she wept in fond memory of her estranged sister, now too late.

Ambi kind of got wind of the situation too; yet he was not mature enough to realize its gravity. As though to truly confirm Indu's absence, he ran up the stairs to her room. With arms akimbo, he inspected the state of the room, as though to truly come to grasp with the fact that his sister was gone.

The black cat that had sat solemnly in a corner jumped towards him, whining softly in a manner that meant 'Indu's gone…Indu's gone.'

It was Ambi who fed Indu's pet kitty that night. As he stood pouring milk in her saucer on the terrace, his father's car arrived.

Kunjammal ran to open the gates. Aware of the inevitable bedlam downstairs, Ambi resolved not to set foot outside Indu's room. The hungry kitten followed him and the milk jug in his hands, purring loudly!

Vijaya likewise kept low, not leaving her room, with the door only slightly ajar to peep!

Only grandma stood bracing her daughter-in-law in defence.

Ramabhadran parked his car, walked in, and plonked onto the sofa, not even up to taking off his coat. Panting for breath, loosening his necktie, he grunted, 'Switch on the fan, will you?'

As the ceiling fan whirred, and whiffs of cool breeze blew, he emitted sounds of utter contentment, and proceeded to address his wife, 'Here, Kunju! No chapatis for me tonight. I had dinner at the club. Of course I hesitated, but Visu insisted, and I gave in, just for today.' He exclaimed so he could be heard all over the neighbourhood. He was always like that. Subtlety was not his forte, nor was stability. He was a man of extremes. Either euphoric with happiness or wild with rage, he lived a man never knowing the need for peace and quiet.

At home, he was his boisterous best. His thick sideburns, feline eyes, his towering stature and resonant voice made for an ominous personality. His mother, petite frame and all, was his only equal in the household, who could at least attempt to quieten him. Nevertheless, his temper was a volatile one and subsided as swiftly as it rose.

'Get my pills now!' he yelled again, taking off his coat. He felt ill-at-ease, having indulged in a forbidden meal. Kunjammal brought his pills and a glass of milk and sat down on the floor, taking his boots off. Ramabhadran popped the pills in his mouth and took a gulp of milk, when his glinting eyes caught sight of the suitcase that stood against a wall. Swallowing the pills, he demanded, 'What's with this suitcase? Why is it here?'

Kunjammal felt the world black out. However, she collected herself in a moment, stepped back a little, and looked up at him with pleading eyes and croaked, 'Indu's gone; he was here and she left along with him…' her sentence stopped midway, as the steel tumbler her husband had held whirred past her ear, hitting the wall beyond, and fell onto the floor ringing madly.

Ramabhadran rose with a towering fury. His eyes glinted as though on fire. 'Where the hell were you all, then?' He cried out. Nobody replied, and nor did he expect them to.

Stamping his foot, he growled, 'She left indeed! Of course, idiots that you are, it's a surprise you both stayed behind. Oh, you wait and see. They can't have gone far. I'll bring both of them to their knees before dawn.'

'Where are you going, now?' demanded grandma.

'Nowhere. I am calling the police,' and he went to the telephone and picked up the receiver.

Kunjammal mustered all her courage and spoke before he began dialing. 'What do you think they can do? She's no more a minor, you see?'

Ramabhadran gave her a sharp look, 'She has ten sovereigns of gold on her. Wasn't that the same pretext with which I reported last time?'

Kunjammal did not let him finish. 'Here, your ten sovereigns of gold. Not a pin have they carried along with them.' And she heaped the handful of jewellery in front of him, and stood boldly.

Ramabhadran brushed them aside impatiently and shouted: 'Idiot woman! Are you teaching me rules of the law? It's for the court to decide whether he was guilty or not. My complaint should be good enough to nab him,' he said with malice, that Kunjammal returned with equal vigour.

'Should that be the case, I shall be in his defence.'

Ramabhadran was taken aback. With the phone in one hand, he stood up furiously, reaching out to smack her head in one blow, when grandma came running in between them.

'Calm down, you devilish man! Think for a moment, with prudence,' she implored.

He however had not shifted his gaze from Kunjammal who stood opposing him, behind his mother.

'Move aside, Amma. How dare she stand up against me?'

Grandma grabbed his hand and shouted back, 'Yes! I am with her as well. So kill me first, will you? I am to blame for Indu's departure. Come on, kill me!' beating her own chest. As his mother exclaimed like an angry goddess, Ramabhadran was stunned into stillness.

His felt his eyes blacking out!

This was sheer betrayal. Such a shocking event carried out by his own mother, faithful wife, and dear children turning into his most bitter enemies, was most unendurable; words failed and choked him, for once.

Shrieking loudly, he seized the telephone off its hook and smashed it on the ground; the next moment his enormous trunk collapsed. Kunjammal rushed forward and held him.

'Ramu, Ramu...' grandma called out to him anxiously.

'Not to worry. He's just knocked out in shock,' Kunjammal comforted her and looked at the broken phone in despair. She shouted out to Ambi. 'Ambi! Run down to the doctor's and fetch him immediately!'

Ambi hurried down the stairs and looked puzzled at his father who now lay sprawled on the sofa. At once, he bolted down the dark street. 'Ambi, wait for me...I'll go with you!' Vijaya followed suit.

Grandma began praying to all the Gods who were part of her daily worship. Kunjammal, looked to her only deity, her wedding necklace, pressing it to her eyes, and waited for the doctor to arrive.

The black kitten scurried outside from the room upstairs, and stood watching the happenings downstairs, with its glinting eyes.

Humans are pretty odd elements indeed, warped and moulded by time. The malleable ones get better moulded with changing times; the brittle ones get broken.

Either way, time does leave its indelible mark on humankind. Is this particular person moulded in a new form with changes over time, or broken irrevocably, or both? That...is for the doctor to say!

A Friend Indeed

'Sir! There's a call for you,' called the office boy. Chandran looked up from his papers. 'For me? Who's calling please?'

'Somebody by the name of Venu, sir,' replied the office boy. Chandran looked up again and his gaze was transfixed on the peon's face. His pen slipped out of his fingers and scrawled on the proof sheets.

'Somebody! Yes, he is somebody indeed,' he firmly repeated to himself.

'Okay, tell him I am not around!'

In the midst of the noisy press, Chandran's ears keenly picked up every word the office boy said to the caller.

'He's not in, sir...No, I don't know...not at his desk. No idea when he'll be back. From Madurai? Yes, I'll tell him. Hotel Jyothi, Room no. 7? Sure, I'll pass on the message.'

As he returned to his cabin, Chandran sat down rubbing his temples.

How did he gather that I have shamelessly returned to work here? It was not yet three months since he had been to Madurai, totally broke, to meet this very Venu, only to face rejection and return devastated.

'How could I forget so soon? And how dare he summon me to his place? Brazen rich kid! Just because he's so wealthy and powerful, he thinks I'm at his beck and call!' Chandran trembled with rage even as these thoughts crossed his mind. Overwhelmed with a sudden desire to call him and lash a few angry words at him, he picked up the phone.

His hand shook with anguish as he held the receiver to his ear.

'Yes, Hotel Jyothi...'

'Please connect me to Room no. 7.'

'Is it room no. 7? May I speak to Mr Venu?' Chandran choked at these words.

'Yes, Venu speaking.' Chandru winced hearing the reply. He found his grit slackening as soon as he heard that voice.

He might not be my friend today. But what a great friend he once was? It turned out to be just fake but how can I deny that it was that fake friendship that paid my tuition fees umpteen times, and attired me royally, to this very shirt that I am wearing right now!

But he changed all of a sudden, for whatsoever reason. Though I threw his money back at him on that fateful day, I had only to sell the watch he had gifted me to meet my expenses and return to Chennai. And although I believe my freedom and respect is being compromised here, I still make my living by working at this job that I have landed, thanks to his influence. Therefore it's not fair that I treat him in the same heartless way he did me. In the few seconds that such varied emotions flocked in his heart, Chandran's face flushed and eyes welled up.

Met with a long silence, the voice on the other end yelled, 'Hello... Hello...'

Chandran's hand stopped shivering. Without a word, he hung up, rubbing his eyes hard to stop the tears from falling.

Chandran and Venu were college buddies. Chandran had no one but his uncle, who died during his first year of college, and he was on the verge of dropping out. Born in one of the wealthiest families in the suburbs of Madurai, Venu had chosen to stay at the college hostel, just to experience the fun and joy of it. He was Chandran's classmate and roommate.

Chandran was a popular orator at the student union meetings. His writings in the college magazine had greatly impressed even the professors. A group of students always thronged about him, with whom he debated about any topic under the sun. Be it political, social, economics, or art, Chandran discussed deeply and articulated his views clearly and firmly. What he hadn't known was that Venu, a sports enthusiast, had been drawn towards him and his knowledge.

After his uncle passed away, Chandran was sadly bidding adieu to his mates as he could no longer pursue his studies; he was leaving Chennai and going to seek a humble living elsewhere. Venu was initially unaware of this. Having taken leave of all his friends, Chandran went to Venu, his roommate, to formally bid him goodbye. Venu was astonished when he learnt why Chandran was leaving.

'Chandru! Do you have any idea how glad and proud I am to be your roommate? Sportspersons are normally the heroes in colleges. But I believe your speeches are more enriching to my mind and soul. I see every day, how much you read and work. Therefore, I know you the best. It will be my personal sorrow if you cease your studies. If there's anything I could do to make you stay, I will be more than happy to do it.' Chandran was completely taken aback by Venu's speech.

'Venu, I had never realized you were so kind. Thank you so much for your kindness. I am at a loss to ask you for any favour. My sole benefactor, my uncle has passed away. I am not in a position that a kind helping hand would solve my troubles. I might have to be a long-term burden. Friendship ought not to be a burden, Venu.' Chandran's eyes moistened.

'Chandru, such favours cannot be a real burden for the affluent. You must accept what I can do for you. Your education shall henceforth be my responsibility, just as it might have been your uncle's, had he lived. I learn more from your talks than the professors' lectures. Allow me to do my bit not to lose that.'

Chandran was dumbfounded. Wrought with emotions, he replied, 'I am so moved that I might actually become a believer and offer my hearty thanks to God!'

'What, so you don't believe in God?' laughed Venu.

'No, I don't,' and Chandran began a vehement lecture on atheism, running late into the night. However, Venu dissented for once. Then he said, 'It's alright, just because we are friends, I don't have to agree with all your views; I am no match to debate with you, so let's agree to disagree!'

'No Venu. We are all science students. We have learnt a lot about evolution theories and about the survival of the fittest. No scientific research has ever come up with even a shred of evidence about God.' At this, they were joined by a few more friends and they all began debating. Venu listened.

From then on, Venu and Chandran became equals not only as students, but in every way of living. Venu shared with Chandran every luxury, every bit of comfort that he himself enjoyed — food, clothes and fun.

When Venu's folks sent him 400 rupees to buy himself a watch, Venu went out and got two watches for 200 each. Chandru winced when Venu insisted him on taking it. 'This is too much', he said, but nevertheless he could not refuse as Venu chided him affectionately.

After four years, they graduated. Venu had on a platter, the job of managing director at his father's new factory in Madurai.

Chandran? What use was his having studied and gained so much knowledge? All he knew was only to explain the ways of the world, not to make his own way through them. Hence, he once again found himself at the verge of his friend's mercy but was too proud to ask. Sensing his reserve, Venu himself said, 'As a friend, it's your right to ask me to help. There is nothing to be ashamed about it. If you are, it only belittles our friendship.'

Chandran was amazed just as he had been several times before. This Venu, who talks so less, has a way with words for sure; so deep and meaningful!

'Ok Venu. It is this. I don't see any future for myself. May I come to Madurai along with you?'

Venu reflected for a moment and replied, 'It isn't proper Chandru; besides, you are not born to work in a factory.' Pondering for a few more moments, he held Chandran's hands and said, 'Don't worry, I am planning something more suitable for you,' and he smiled.

In a few days, Venu called Chandran, excited. 'Chandru! I have found the right job for you. A friend of my father's is starting a daily newspaper on a grand scale. I have no doubt that journalism is indeed your calling. I told him all about you and he consented immediately. You can join them this very month!' Venu bubbled with happiness for his friend and the success of his own efforts. Chandran felt overjoyed, albeit a bit nervous, at becoming a journalist for such a big daily.

In the next five years, Chandran and Venu were in constant correspondence through letters. Venu followed all of Chandran's articles, and would write to him expressing his pride and joy. During his frequent business visits to Chennai they would meet, and when Venu shopped for expensive clothes in the city, he would get Chandran similar ones too. Much against Chandran's protests, he also gave him enough money to spend. All this was not only because the factory was flourishing under him and he was making a lot of money, but also because Venu was generous by nature and his heart only felt contented in giving things away.

'Just because I am his friend, I get to enjoy such luxuries that only he can afford. However, I don't get to share any of the burdens or work pressure his crucial position demands of him,' Chandran mused.

Six months ago, Venu got married. He was naturally donning the finest of designer suits on his wedding. Chandran had only casually quipped how handsome the groom looked in his finery. That did it. Venu got a bee in his bonnet that he must get Chandran the same suit as soon as possible.

'Chandru. Get married soon. I'll take care of your wedding suit.'

'Thank goodness. Had I got married, listening to him, what a sorry state things would have been in? Especially last month when I quit my job and he turned cold towards me.' He also mulled, 'Could his new wife be the reason behind his sudden change of heart?'

Last month, Chandran had had a tiff with his boss. His boss had asked him to write an editorial welcoming the launch of a new retrograde political party.

'No, I won't!' refused Chandran, who was highly antagonistic towards the party.

'Well lad, the paper is mine. Your job is to write what I bid you to,' replied his boss.

'I cannot write anything against my ideologies. Isn't a writer entitled to his freedom of expression?' Chandran was stubborn.

'Mr Chandran, freedom of expression and ideologies are the privileges of freelance authors. You are a journalist on my payroll!'

'Sir, enough is enough. You have made it clear how much you respect writing and writers. I quit!' Chandran hastily scribbled a resignation letter and left with an air of utmost annoyance.

'What gave me such audacity? Well, I ought not to have angered a capitalist just because I was friends with another. That's the lesson I learnt then,' Chandran thought bitterly.

After quitting his job, Chandran had written twice to Venu but to his amazement, Venu had not replied. Finally, he decided to go to Madurai and meet him, with a mere 15 rupees in his pocket. He was totally counting on Venu for even lodging and other expenses.

It was well past 11 am when he reached Madurai that morning, so he directly went to Venu's office, instead of his residence.

He waited for a long time at the office reception, flipping through glossy business magazines, when a peon finally called him inside. Chandran was awed as he stepped into Venu's posh office. Hiding his intimidation at his 'friend's' powerful position and affecting joviality, Chandran said, 'Hey Venu! I was wondering why you never wrote back to me. So, I thought I'd come and check on you myself!'

'Oh, I have been really busy. I am leaving for Kodaikanal right now for a fortnight's stay. My wife has long been insisting on this vacation but things have been so hectic until now.' Venu offhandedly shrugged his shoulders and adjusted his necktie. He was not even looking at Chandran. Chandran could not make out this sudden change in his friend's behaviour. But he could comprehend just one thing; this millionaire was clearly upset that Chandran had upset another.

A short silence fell in their midst. Chandran continued to ponder. 'How fickle are human minds? Is this Venu talking to me like this? I never knew he was even up to such high-and-mighty ways. He is not even looking at my face while talking to me; such offhanded airs and graces! Oh, it's the way of the wealthy. It's how the rich behave. Well, it suits him, I should admit. But I have come this far; let me ask him this one last favour as a friend's right and then take his leave forever.'

'Venu, you know I have quit my job…'

'Oh yes, you had written all about it…' Venu lit a cigarette. 'I don't think you have done right.' He let out a whirl of smoke.

Chandran was piqued. 'Do you expect me to give up my ideals and conscience and write against my principles?'

'Ideals, conscience, principles…Haven't you learnt to talk practically, yet?' smiled Venu.

'Just because I am employed, should I be a slave or what?' asked a flustered Chandran.

Venu pursed his lips. 'Well, Chandru. It is your personal affair. You can do as you please. My goodness! It's already one.' Venu glanced at his watch. 'I must be leaving home by half-past one. Please make haste and let me know the purpose of your visit.'

Chandran's heart wrenched at Venu's new attitude of shrugging of shoulders and pursing of lips, the brushing aside of 'his personal affair', and the fact that his only friend was so contemptuous of his visit.

However, he took his friend's last advice and decided to be 'practical'. 'I came to seek your help. Let this be the last trouble I give you. I am completely broke after I quit my job. I'll soon find employment with some other firm. But until then…' Chandran stammered and switched over to English, hoping that his request could sound less shameless in a non-native language.

Venu hung his head and listened. He was flexing his fingers and rubbing his forehead all the while.

'Wasn't it you who had once told me? One should not be ashamed to seek favours from a friend and such bashfulness is shameful. I bear that in mind when I ask you this. You promised me that expensive suit. I don't want that. Instead give me half the cost of that suit. It would suit me better now!' Chandran blurted out blushing furiously, but managing to smile as well.

With an unmistakable air of a blatant lie, and affecting a totally foreign manner, Venu spoke; he didn't sound like himself at all when he said these words: 'I don't have any money on me right now; will see you around.' With these words of utter negligence, Venu rose from his seat.

Chandran followed him in a trance, trying to gather his own shattered self. Venu's office boy opened the doors for his boss. Chandran walked behind him; he saw Venu's chauffeur waiting with the car door held open. As an aristocratic Venu walked smartly towards his car, Chandran carrying his humble travel bag, felt the ground slip beneath his feet.

'Ok, you go home. Will see you later.' Venu climbed into his car. Just as the car started, he called Chandru back. 'Do you have money for the bus?' He handed 20 rupees to him. Chandran's arms stretched involuntarily too. As both of them realized this involuntary act on either side, the two notes fell on Venu's face with Chandran's angry words, 'Thank you very much.' And he walked away.

Chandran could only comprehend Venu's sudden change in attitude thus: 'A capitalist himself, his loyalty lies with that right-wing retrograde party. No wonder he has disowned me for his own political reasons.'

However, Chandru had to sell his watch, gifted once by Venu, to make ends meet and return to Chennai. Finding another job was no breeze as he had imagined. It was not before an ordeal of a whole month that his ex-employer, who got wind of his hardships, decided to give him another chance. So, he met Chandru 'by chance' at a party.

'This is a democratic country; you journalists are, of course, entitled to your own opinions and ideologies; however, you have to understand that this democracy supports capitalism, and as a capitalist, I cannot encourage your freedom of speech to encroach into mine, can I? After all the paper is mine, boss! Therefore, as long as you're working at my paper, you have got to write what goes down well with me. May I suggest something, though? Why don't you leftist journalists form a union and bring out your own paper, as in West Bengal? It works like this. Whatever you write in my paper, according to my bidding, you could utterly counteract in yours. How's that? However, I doubt if it would work here, where revolutionary journalists like you, are rare and few. Most of them are mercenary wretches.' Chandru who was listening, felt those last words touching a nerve.

Therefore, swallowing his pride, he rejoined the paper and began working in earnest. Moreover, he had begun the ground work of rounding up like-minded people and starting his own revolutionary paper, eventually a revolution! Ah, how much easier are dreams to talk about.

❋

Chandru returned to his room around six in the evening and found Venu sitting on a stool outside his locked door, waiting for him. 'I've been expecting you for about half an hour,' smiled Venu.

Chandru could not even bring himself to look at his face. He was looking down as he opened the door.

'Chandru, you seem to have lost a lot of weight, been overworking, have you?' Venu lightly touched Chandru's shoulder. Chandru brushed his hands away and walked inside. Only after the few moments that passed as he removed his shirt, did he realize that Venu was still standing outside, expecting to be invited inside. Chandru felt bad.

'Come in,' he said formally.

Venu came in, and placed the carton that he had brought with him on Chandru's cot, switched on the lights and sat down on a chair. With a huge sigh, he removed his coat and loosened his tie. Chandru saw him sweating and switched on the fan. However, he could not bring himself to talk to Venu.

Venu decided to break the ice by asking Chandru for cigarettes, though he very well had some in his own coat pocket. Chandru opened a cigarette packet and handed it to Venu. As Venu thanked him, Chandru's eyes welled up. 'Hey Venu, what has become of us? How could our friendship fade into such fake civility?' he thought.

'Chandru, you must be really mad at me, eh?' Venu finally asked him, with a smile.

'Oh, who am I to be? And how does it matter to you, anyway?' Chandru hung his head.

'Come on, I know you must be really mad at me. After all, I am guilty of dismissing a friend who came to me when needy, am I not?'

Chandru gave him a fiery look 'Friendship? That's far behind us now, I am afraid.'

'Hey, Chandru, that reminds me of your recent story, "A friend". I know, the antagonist was based on me but I don't mind at all. I think those are the perks of being a writer. Even misunderstanding somebody gives you a gift of a character!'

'Literary characters are but born out of the people we meet in life. Although, we have been the best of friends, you cannot deny that we belong to different classes. It's no surprise that you were hostile towards me, who opposed the party that favoured the interests of your class...' Chandru paused as he found Venu laughing heartily.

'Oh, go on Chandru, go on. It's been so long since I heard you talk. And that's exactly why I am here, having cancelled a business trip and all. But please do not sign me up into that party without my permission! Get your facts straight bro! I am the only industrialist who is dead against that retrograde party in Madurai. I think you should know that...' So saying, Venu took off his shirt, hung it on a hanger and wrapped his shoulders with one of Chandru's towels.

Chandru was perplexed now. He could now find no other explanation for Venu's erratic behaviour on that fateful day.

Venu sensed this. He drew a chair near to Chandru and collected his own thoughts, determined to set things right between them, to explain everything to Chandru. However, he first popped a cigarette in his mouth and lit it with the one Chandru was smoking, ignoring the lighter in his pocket! Then, he cleared his throat and began:

'Chandru, let me not beat about the bush. I am not a great orator like you. But I hope I can make things clear to you. Chandru, you always believed life was a battle. I only wanted you to fight your own. You have said in your story that friendships across classes can only be fleeting. I foresaw this even before you did, and wanted to spare our friendship the dishonour.'

Chandru now looked up disbelievingly. But he rose from the cot on which he had been lying down till then.

'Yes, sit down beside me, and I'll explain.' Venu pulled a chair for him.

'I have a lot of friends within my own class and society; they all carry some sort of hidden interest, business, social, or political. You are the only one with whom I have enjoyed friendship in its true spirit.

Such a friendship is a man's greatest gift. It needs nothing but like-mindedness and love. I have even met quite a few friends like that. But unfortunately, I am born rich. So I was always bound to "help" them when they came to me in need, and I did so, gladly, as I felt that was the right thing to do. Of course, it was no trouble for me at all, but it gradually crippled them. And I felt bad because I felt they were my friends merely because I was supporting them. We all have our own battles to fight, don't we? And it's our duty to face them head on. So at times when I put mine before theirs, those friends turned against me; they believed I had shown my true colours, the colours of my class! And so went our friendships down the drain. You remained my only friend then. I thought about all of this, when you came to me, that day, seeking help. And if I am not wrong, you wouldn't have thrown away your job like that, had I not been your friend, would you?'

Chandru bit his lip, realizing the truth in Venu's words.

'So I thought long and hard about you, Chandru,' continued Venu. 'I felt it best to give you a chance to fight your own troubles. I was afraid that my friendship would turn you into a mere puppet who is all tall talk but has never faced any action. If it did, our friendship was sure to fail as well. Just think, if I had given you the money you had asked for, I would have only encouraged you into more such impulsive and irresponsible acts. Whereas now, you have resumed your job here, and not only that, you are working brilliantly to realize your dreams as well. I know of many frivolous people who are contented to just talk all day about lofty ideologies but are not even up to taking care of themselves. I couldn't stand by and let you become one of them, for such people are not even worthy of simple friendships, leave alone great dreams.'

'Now, you haven't lost your freedom of speech by working for that capitalist paper. You are working alongside to bring your own journal.

If you had quit that job, it would have been nothing short of dodging trouble. That's exactly why I asked you to "stay practical". Is it enough to merely pronounce "life is a battle"? You got to truly realize it; only then can you find your ways through it. Is it fair that you ask me to fight your battle? Is it worthy of a self-confident individual like you? It is important to stand on your own, fight for yourself; that's the foremost thing in life; friendship is but secondary. Moreover, you have yourself said: friendship ought not to be a burden, right?' smiled Venu.

Chandru's heart felt much lighter too. He wanted to smile back at Venu, but his lips quivered with unsaid emotions.

'I learnt from my mistakes with others. That's why I thought of getting into your bad books before it was too late, so I may have enough time to make amends when the time is right! I knew what I did, so I am not going to apologize for however badly I may have behaved that day,' smiled Venu.

Chandru felt a glow of pride for his friend as he imbibed all of Venu's wise words. Finally he spoke. 'Well, I am not going to ask for your forgiveness either. Because I know you already have,' he said smilingly.

'My goodness. I swear I reconcile with my wife with a lot less trouble than this. All evening, I have struggled to see this smile on your face! Well, here's the suit that you liked so much.' Venu opened the box and displayed the gift he had brought for his friend. 'Remember you asked for half the price of this suit that day. Now please take any amount of money you might need, along with this suit,' saying this, he took out his wallet too.

'Oh, I don't need anything.' Chandru shrugged.

'Hey, Chandru, these are just mementoes of our friendship, not the foundation. After all, it's money, the most trivial of things. Never make it a big deal by asking for or refusing it.'

Chandru heard these words and joyously extended his hand. Throwing aside his wallet, Venu rushed forward. As the two dear friends firmly held hands, sealing their pact of friendship, the expensive suit and money lay at their feet, claiming their rightful place of least importance.

THE TRUTH

Somanathan was embarrassed to see that portrait hung on the wall. Adjusting his glasses, he drew close to the wall and peered, to find his picture, right between that of Swami Vivekananda and Ramakrishna Paramahamsa; he grimaced.

It was just then, that his niece Kodhai returned from the kitchen, bringing him a cup of Horlicks. 'Who put this up here?' Somanathan asked her, pointing to his picture on the wall.

Kodhai set the cup upon the coffee table and moved towards the wall. 'Oh, it's the way things are, ever since I came here. "They are my revered godfathers," he tells his friends, and that's what he told me as well!' Somanathan chuckled; removing his glasses and wiping them with his shawl, he said, 'What an irony this is, for sure! An atheist as myself put on par with religious stalwarts?' Shaking his head in disbelief, he made his way towards the sofa, tapping his walking stick.

Kodhai handed him the cup of Horlicks. He took it in his shivering old hands and drank deeply. Finding beads of sweat covering his forehead, Kodhai got up to switch on the fan. A thick tuft of grey hair brushed his forehead. Somanathan looked around, his keen eyes taking in every detail of the living room, the radio, the statue of Buddha in one corner, the pale blue curtains, finally landing upon the face of his niece. He smiled at her kindly, his eyes shining with child-like fervour.

That smile said it all: A praise, 'Smart girl, the house looks very well-kept'; an enquiry, 'I hope you are happy, my child!' and a proud declaration, 'I am so happy to see you!'

As a reply to all of the above, Kodhai smiled back with utmost decorum and the virtue of her femininity. Somanathan looked at his watch and exclaimed, 'Oh, it is five. Is he this long usually? My train is at seven.'

At the same moment, Kodhai hurried towards the gates, as she heard them open. Somanathan stood up in anticipation, to embrace Parameswaran.

Kodhai came back in, an envelope in hand, 'It was the postman, and there's a letter for him.'

Somanathan picked up a photo album, and began flipping through the pictures, as he sat waiting for Parameswaran.

❊

Ten years ago Somanathan taught English at the same college in which Parameswaran now teaches Tamil. In the brief period when Parameswaran, a student, transformed into a colleague of his own professor Somanathan, there developed a special bond between the two. After retirement, Somanathan retired to his hometown, but they occasionally corresponded through letters. Two years ago, when Somanathan had come to Chennai on personal grounds, he met Parameswaran for the first time in 10 years, and he was quite astonished; not only because his young student had looked so altered as a respected professor — tweed coat, glasses, greying temples and all, but because, at 40, he remained a confirmed bachelor.

Parameswaran was delighted to meet his idol and greeted him with utmost reverence. Somanathan embraced him with equal warmth and said, 'I am disconcerted seeing that you haven't yet married. Should I be worried?'

Somanathan was always firm and sound in his convictions. However, he seldom stated them with a challenging air. He always ended his statements with a question, open for discussion, inviting a healthy exchange of views. This, as Parameswaran knew, was a commendable virtue of his mentor.

Parameswaran had no next of kin to claim. Matrimony for such modest single men could only be a distant dream, but for kind friends, who must then duly carry out the 'match-making' activity. Parameswaran realized that Somanathan, his beloved friend and mentor was anxious, more so because he believed it was his duty.

'Is celibacy a vice, sir?' Parameswaran smilingly questioned his mentor.

'It's neither a vice nor a virtue. If celibacy is not for a cause loftier than itself, it's not only irrational but also highly incorrect. If you choose to stay chaste for a substantial reason, I shall stop worrying.'

Parameswaran seemed lost in thought; not exactly — he was amazed! A smile appeared on his face; not exactly — he had surrendered!

They both then engaged in a long conversation. Parameswaran, now a mature man in his middle age, could much appreciate his mentor's wisdom, and felt more drawn towards him than ever before.

On the day of his departure, Somanathan invited Parameswaran to visit him at his hometown.

'I extend this invitation with a sense of duty. I would like you to meet my niece; she is like a daughter to me, having lost her parents at an early age. She was a confirmed spinster too, but recently I find her mind attuned towards marriage. It shall be my obligation to marry you both, if there is mutual consent and liking.' Parameswaran was overwhelmed at his mentor making him an offer of matrimony, purely on the basis of friendship and goodwill, disregarding societal pressures of caste or creed.

And two years ago, they were married, not before Parameswaran had to overcome a mental hurdle. He was concerned that Kodhai was 20 while he was 40.

Sensing this, Somanathan said, 'It is quite alright if you do not want to get married to someone younger by a score of years. Even though, there is no reason to believe it could be a snag, it will be purely at your discretion.'

Parameswaran was baffled. He was unable to make an emphatic statement. He was aware that Somanathan would neither coerce him nor take offense, should he decline to marry Kodhai.

Somanathan inferred that Parameswaran's hesitation was not deeply felt, and that the latter had made up his mind in favour of the marriage. Somanathan asked him gently, 'What's your problem, really?'

Parameswaran blushed like a school boy and said, 'Well, our respective ages…'

'Ohhh!' Somanathan laughed out loud. 'Well, as I already said, if it really bothers you, we shall drop the idea. But, worrying over mindless gossip is unnecessary and insensible.'

'Well, one must think a little of the world.'

'Why little, think through thoroughly. However, what is to be given due thought, matters. The world does not revolve around our narrow boundaries. In several societies of this world, these differences matter little in love or marriage; in fact much preferred. If you do not wish to seek justification from a broader perspective as that, then why seek one from a narrow neighbourhood? Better validate your own feelings as an individual, and make a decision,' Somanathan replied and fell into thoughtful silence.

Parameswaran was awed. How deeply he studies a fellow man's mind?

Somanathan continued, 'A man normally marries for his own interests, and so does a woman. Selfish interests inevitably bring dissatisfaction. The essence of marriage is anything but selfish. Marriage is a sacrament by which an individual stops living in one's own terms, and begins living for another. Selfless and noble civilized life must begin within the family — the fundamental unit of this society. However, men and women marry for selfish motives, seeking only their own happiness, thereby hindering home peace, which is ultimately detrimental to the society. Therefore think not, that this marriage is for your sake; rather it's for hers; and I have told her that it's for your sake. A solid relationship must be founded on such sentiments, right?'

Parameswaran looked lost; not really — he was astounded!

※

His past two years of blissful matrimony had taught him the true meaning of life. His bond with Kodhai had strengthened such that he could not imagine a life without her; she had seen to it! She was his soul mate in every sense. Henceforth, he naturally felt a lot more deference to his mentor who made such wholesome happiness possible and loved his wife, dearer than life.

His belief in their happy marriage was reinforced after his conversation with Kodhai one night, when he casually broached the subject of their ages.

In one of their most intimate moments, as she lay close to him, stroking his chest, her lips brushing his earlobes, her words gave him tingling goose-bumps.

'Well, I was just as hesitant as you were. But...but now I believe that this is the ideal age difference between couples for a blissful marriage. Couples with the same age could be egoistical and unforgiving. Well, I don't know, I somehow believe, this disparity in our ages is the reason I am...really happy, really happy!' When she had finished speaking her carefully chosen words that expressed exactly what she felt, both their hearts brimmed with joy.

The photo album on their coffee table carried pictures of them posing together against backdrops ranging from the lakes of Kashmir to the rivers of Kanyakumari — a direct evidence to their happy marriage.

As Somanathan flipped through the last leaf of the album and shut it contentedly, he found Parameswaran at the front door, smiling at him with palms held together in respect. 'Welcome, sir. When did you arrive?'

Somanathan smiled back innocuously, shook the younger man's hands and heartily patted him on the back.

'Well, I was here today on business. Leaving by the seven o' clock train.' Parameswaran looked disappointed. 'It's five-thirty already. Alright, I'll see you off on your train,' and looked at his watch.

'Oh, what's the hurry? There's still plenty of time. We can start after you have freshened up and had your tea.'

Parameswaran however could lose no time away from his idol. He dawdled about, removing his coat, not taking his eyes off the elder man. Kodhai came and took his coat away and handed him a towel. Parameswaran threw it upon his shoulders and sat down on the sofa to take off his boots. Somanathan asked him, 'I am greatly amused at this weird arrangement,' he pointed to the pictures on the wall.

'What's there to be amused about? One of them taught me unflinching faith; another the greatness of celibacy, and the one in the centre helped me find the essence of life. They are all my venerable idols.'

'Oh, this is too much. You flatter me exaggeratedly.' Somanathan shrugged his shoulders and smiled.

'No, I humbly worship you.' Parameswaran replied solemnly.

'I do not believe in any form of worship,' grimaced Somanathan.

'It's not the idol who needs faith, but the devotee. I draw my inner strength out of this. Do you mind, sir?' and he went inside.

'Oh, what a sentimental man!' murmured Somanathan.

In a short while, Parameswaran reappeared, clad in a clean white dhoti and shirt, with sacred ash smeared across his forehead. Kodhai handed him his tea and the letter, as he sat down. Parameswaran finished his tea and opened the letter.

To Professor Parameswaran!

Before you ignore this anonymous letter, be aware that even anonymous letters can be eye-openers.

Your life is founded upon betrayal and lies. Your venerable idol Mr Somanathan — you know not what a conman he is. Your beloved Kodhai, in whose love you rejoice, you know nothing about her horrific past! She was abandoned by her lover when she got pregnant. And then, as fate would have it, or Mr Somanathan's advice would, she had a miscarriage. Your mentor has clearly hoodwinked you into marrying her. While ignorance may be bliss, remember that you are only making a fool of yourself.

Parameswaran's instant reaction was to shred the letter into a zillion bits. However, checking himself in a moment, he folded it and put it his pocket.

'Anything important?' Somanathan asked enquiringly.

'Oh, nothing,' Parameswaran managed a false smile. He resolved with all his might to forget all about the letter and say nothing of it. His eyes traversed on to the pictures on the wall, his beloved Kodhai who stood beside like an angel, and finally landed on Somanathan whose inquisitive gaze had not yet faltered. Parameswaran suspected whether his mentor was reading his mind, by the way he was keenly watching him.

Reading discomfort from his face, Kodhai came near him, 'Do you have a headache?'

'No,' and he looked up; his eyes were red and moist. 'You look feverish; probably running a temperature,' she felt his forehead.

'Here, let me see,' and Somanathan walked up to him and touched his forehead.

'Well, I think you are just tired and probably take rest. Let me take leave. I shall return next week and stay a couple of days.' He patted the younger man on the back.

'There's nothing wrong with me; some fresh air will do me good. I shall come and see you off; give me a minute please.' Parameswaran smiled with difficulty and rose to go inside. He checked his appearance in the mirror, strolled for a few moments on the terrace, all in an effort to compose himself. The words 'Even anonymous sources can be eye-openers' and 'Your life is founded upon betrayal and lies' weighed heavily within his pocket. He could neither believe nor ignore them. Suddenly, as if challenging the letter, he asked himself, 'Well, so what? What do I care about Kodhai's past? She is now my devoted wife and our marriage, impeccable. Must a sinner be doomed for life?' With his will and sense bracing him, the letter fluttered in his hands. Had his grip loosened, it could have been lost forever, however his fingers firmly clutched it. He felt both a strong urge to tear it into pieces, as well as to hold it tightly.

'This letter speaks about my wife. Whether it's the truth or just a prank, it can't hurt the bond we share. Yes, I cannot live without her. I don't care about the past.' Fiercely determined, he stared into the skies. The next moment, he winced, his eyes narrowed. A voice from within whispered. 'Oh, but I must know the truth. I must!' This tiny thought grew to such enormity that it engulfed him in a moment. 'Oh, what a shame! How this tiny letter torments me!' As he picked it up with a will to destroy it, once again, his fingers stopped midway. A quarter of the letter was torn. The torn part spoke, 'Anonymous letters can be eye-openers too'.

'Are you now? As soon as it comes to light that you are nothing but some green-eyed monster's cruel mischief, Kodhai and I will together rip you to pieces. Else, we shall make a bonfire of you declaring our victory over the past demons.'

'But, how am I to know the truth? Is this letter the purpose of his visit? To explain it away?' with this idea, he hurried down the steps.

In the taxi, on their way to the railway station, Parameswaran broke the silence. 'You have known me for so long; you also are well aware of the blessed life I lead with Kodhai, all thanks to you.' Unable to say anymore, he took the letter from his pocket.

Somanathan was startled. Parameswaran switched on the tiny light within the taxi and handed him the letter. 'Without much ado, just tell me if this letter speaks the truth or a lie. Just that. Whatever you may say shall have no bearing upon anything or anyone, I swear.' Somanathan saw that Parameswaran's fingers were trembling as he held out the letter. He took it and began reading it quite nonchalantly. Parameswaran's gaze was fixed on his mentor's face. 'I just want to know the truth. That's all,' he added, quite perturbed.

Somanathan smiled at him, again innocuously, as though to mock at him, saying, 'Such curiosity only goes to show how fallible you are!' and he patted his back and said, 'I never knew you were so emotional. This is quite unhealthy; you are sure to become hypertensive!'

'I am dying to seek the truth,' pleaded Parameswaran.

'Seek the truth? That's none of our business, but of sanyasins!' Somanathan smiled at the younger man.

Parameswaran was now slightly miffed with Somanathan's dawdling; yet he stayed composed.

'Mr Parameswaran, you must realize that this letter's motive is pure malice and baseness,' Somanathan began. Parameswaran interrupted him, adamantly. 'I entreat you to reply in a single word, whether this is to be believed or not.'

Sensing the firmness in his voice, and empathizing with the underlying feelings, Somanathan asked, 'In a single word?' he looked up at Parameswaran's face.

'Yes, and I will believe whatever you shall say.'

Somanathan laughed disbelievingly, as the promise sounded childlike and intoxicated.

'I am upset that this letter should disturb and transform you in this way. Well, listen. I reply to you in a single word. It's a LIE.' His lips quivered as he handed back the letter to Parameswaran.

Neither of them spoke a word thereon. Even as he boarded the train and took leave, Somanathan had not uttered a word after 'LIE'.

However, Parameswaran could not help thinking that it was just that single word that rang untrue. The next moment he felt ashamed of the thought. 'Oh, how mean and despicable has this letter turned me? It's a grave mistake that I even discussed this with him. How lowly he must think of me, now?' Thus regretting his rash action, Parameswaran returned home.

As he entered the house, he found that Kodhai had gone upstairs to their bedroom. Usually, he would seek her out. Today, he just flopped onto the sofa staring at the pictures on the wall.

Kodhai who was waiting for him in vain, came back downstairs to the living room. 'What's the matter? Are you alright?' She felt his forehead again. It felt normal. Parameswaran grabbed her hand, his own trembling.

'What...what happened to you?' Kodhai was startled as she lifted up his chin; her husband's face was wrought with pain, as he looked up, almost in tears; his eyes implored. At the same time, he thought, 'What a fool I am! Here stands my beloved wife, who is incapable of deceiving me in any way. Why should I torment myself, when I can ask her directly?'

Putting on a cheerful face, he said, 'Oh, I am perfectly alright. Won't you sit down? There is something that troubles me. Only you can put an end to it. You know me enough to know that I cannot live without you, no matter what.' He choked at these words. 'Here, read this. I seek no explanation but only if this is true or not. Whatever you might have to say will alter nothing. That's a promise! I only ask to know the truth. I want to believe that my life was not based upon lies.' As he kept talking even after handing her the letter, she had quietly finished reading it. Closing her eyes and bracing herself, she said in a clear and firm voice. 'It's true.'

Parameswaran was astounded, as she continued, 'It was a grave mistake in my life, for which there's none to be blamed. I had resigned to my fate ever since, determined to live a lonely and weary life. My uncle however, was relentless in convincing me otherwise. It was then that I met you and agreed to marry you. My uncle had said, "It's pointless to revive the ghosts of the past. Let bygones be bygones. Certain truths can have a scorching effect on people; and very few can bear the burn."'

'Well, I never meant to keep secrets from you, nor deliberately deceive you. As your wife, I did not have the heart to lie to you even after being confronted. This was my chance to make a clear breast of it. You might be shocked, for this is a singular and bitter truth from the past. But I believe you are up to enduring it.'

Parameswaran had tears in his eyes. He suddenly grew livid at Somanathan, as he screamed his blazing heart out. 'I forgive you, Kodhai! But, I can never forgive that man who had been utterly dishonest with me even a while back, when I had confronted him with complete trust. Oh, I shall never forgive his betrayal, NEVER!' and he jumped up from the sofa and ran towards the pictures on the wall; tearing off the centremost portrait, the one that adorned his most revered position, and threw it on the floor. It fell across the living room, into a corner, the glass smashing to smithereens. 'Ha, great philosopher indeed!' he swore under his breath. Kodhai could hear him dashing to his room upstairs and slamming it shut.

'Oh, the truth has hurt indeed!' murmured Kodhai.

Disillusioned and deeply hurt, Parameswaran lay still on his bed, not up to facing anything or anybody. The door was knocked, but he did not stir; he waited for another knock and as it never came, he rose and opened the door.

There stood Kodhai, suitcase in hand, ready to leave. Their eyes met in a deep gaze that lasted several seconds. Kodhai said, 'I have always felt that your devotion to my uncle was extreme. But now seeing your display of utter disregard for him, I come to realize his profound wisdom and his great ability to see every dark corner of the human mind. He was fully aware that truth could hurt and you cannot stand to bear it. You know, your forgiving me is nothing but deceiving yourself. If you deem it an offense, you ought to punish me. Well, you cannot, because you are not that strong. However, you are unable to put it behind you and so you punish uncle. It's no different from a rebuked child, taking it out on its younger sibling. Your inability to punish me is nothing more than a sign of your weakness, rather selfishness. Either way, living together anymore is going to be a penalty for both of us. I hold no grudge against you; I am going to seek his pardon for having disregarded his wise words and bringing great hurt and damage to a hapless soul.' Without waiting for a reply, Kodhai turned around and descended the staircase. Parameswaran watched her in silence.

'Seek the truth? That's none of our business, but of sanyasins!' Parameswaran recalled Somanathan's light-hearted words, reflecting on their profundity.

Parameswaran was lost in thought; well not exactly—he was astounded! A smile appeared on his face; not exactly—it was a sign of surrender.

He rushed down the staircase to find Kodhai leaving through the front door and called out to her.

She turned around and this was what she saw: Parameswaran was hanging his mentor's portrait back on its due place on the wall, and he turned to smile fondly at his wife.

Well, if he could forgive and someone who had lied to him, not to mention idolize him as before, would he not forgive his beloved wife, the one who had been admirably candid with him?

THE MASQUERADE

Part I

'Is it 11 am already? Kumaran, on your way back from the bank, go to our Chidambaram annachi's store, take him aside if it's crowded, and remind him about his due to us. He promised us as early as last Friday; let him know we are in need, now.' With these words, Chettiyar turned around to find the little boy in a corner of the textile showroom dozing over the cloth bales. Chettiyar picked up a yardstick, tiptoed towards the boy and hit him squarely on his forehead. The little boy woke up with a jolt and hastily rubbed his now throbbing head, fear and pain overwhelming him.

'Hey boy! Sleeping in broad daylight, are we?'

The boy was dumbfounded.

'Come here, will you?' Chettiyar growled and the boy began to sob, trying to stop the tears with the back of his palm.

Unperturbed by this drama, Kumaran stood right beside them, counting the stacks of currency and placing them carefully in his leather money bag. After all, the little boy is a shadow of his past; he couldn't care less, even if he tried. But his thoughts did not spare Sampath, who sat inside, grinning stupidly; 'Of course he finds it funny; the rich moron, son of a government officer.'

'Mr Chettiyar, please try and make a man out of my stupid boy; a total failure at school and has bad company to boot.' Chettiyar was only too happy to indulge the 20-year old lad.

'Sir!' he said to the officer, 'He's but a child! Give him some time, and he'll soon get skilled enough to manage a shop on his own.'

Sampath got an honorary pay of 30 rupees per month.

'Well, well, laugh idiot!' Kumaran mumbled under his breath, throwing him a glare, that he missed but Chettiyar did not.

The boy was still crying.

'Hey little fellow! Is it right to sleep at work?' Chettiyar asked him genially now.

The boy still could not reply.

'Is it right?' Chettiyar's voice grew stern now.

'No, sir!' came the meek reply.

'Will you sleep again?'

'No, sir!'

'Here, go have some tea, wash your face, and get me some betel leaves. Okay?' and he slammed a quarter *anna* on the table.

The boy wiped his face with his shirt, took the change and turned to go.

'Oh come on, why the long face, taking the money and all? Come on, give us a smile, will you?'

The boy managed a weak smile across his tear-stricken face. He felt mildly cheerful at the thought of getting some tea.

'Here, have you counted the cash? Four thousand alright? Do be careful to deposit the amount and return as soon as possible. Once you're back, send Sampath home for lunch, even if I am not around.'

Kumaran nodded vaguely in reply, slipped on his chappals that lay beneath the wooden porch, and stepped onto the street; he stopped for a moment to wonder, 'Which way to go, now?'

Now, there were three routes that could take one from ALK Chettiyar textiles that stood on West Raja street, generally referred to as Big Bazaar Street, to the bank on East Raja Street.

One could step out of the shop, turn left round the corner, and walk down the South Street towards the bank; or take right, turn again, and walk down the South Street. The third route was to pass through the hatchway of the temple courtyard gates flanked on both sides by shops that sold trinkets. Through the hatchway, one could enter the temple grounds, take half a stroll around the temple, and exit through the east fort gates to reach the bank facing right opposite — apparently the shortest route to the bank. Nevertheless, Kumaran always walked down the South Street for several reasons. One — it was always too hot to walk barefoot, as one must within the temple premises; two — it was on the nook joining the East and South Street that the big temple-car platform stood. And there, spending all his time gambling or flirting with the fruit-hawker women, would be Veeran, Kumaran's childhood chum. It was customary for Kumaran to tip him for tea. Also, there was Kamatchi Vilas where Kumaran usually lunched; so it was always the South Street route for him.

So why the unusual dilly-dallying today? Fifteen years ago, he was hired as a small boy for odd jobs such as fetching water, sweeping the floor, being tirelessly at Chettiyar's beck and call, stealing only moments to nap, leaning against walls. Smart and diligent, he soon became one of the able shop assistants, cleverly bargained with customers and grew to be the most responsible and trusted associate of Chettiyar himself. Rain or sunshine, umpteen times he'd run to the bank and never once had he wondered which way to go.

After a few seconds, he suddenly turned to look at the shop. Chettiyar who was rummaging for something in his desk did not notice him. Sampath who sat across was still watching Kumaran with keen interest.

'Oh, just you wait, morons! You good-for-nothing idiot get the same pay as I do; how fair is that? Well, you're not to blame, but Chetty is; to hell with you both!' Gritting his teeth, Kumaran swiftly entered the temple gate hatchway, a route he seldom took.

'What about Veeran?'

'Damn! Must I think of him just now? I'd rather pray for my own safety and seek the Lord's blessings.' As he exited the temple through the gates of the east fort, he quickened his stride, keeping his head down to avoid anyone familiar, such as Veeran. The money bag tucked under his arm felt unusually heavy. He opened it, took out a hundred rupee note and put it in his pocket. Then, shutting the bag and buttoning it, he wrapped it with his hand-towel, tucking it casually like a bundle of drapes, under his arm.

But where?

Where is he off to now, passing by the bank, and on to the next street?

Just a few moments ago, until he took those steps beyond the bank — the crime, the betrayal, was just namesake — a design, a fantasy. After all, he was allowed possession of the money only as far as the bank, whatever detours he might take. Every step he took beyond that could take him to any lengths of doom and misery.

Yes, he was now a thief!

Kumaran? A thief? Say that aloud and there'll be a public outcry at the Bazaar Street. Nevertheless, he was certainly a thief now.

'Is this me? Am I doing this? Am I no different from Veeran? Oh no, I can't do this. It's not too late yet; I should just go back to the bank right now.' Panting for breath and sweating profusely, he kept walking though.

'I think 4,000 should be more than enough…to go to a faraway town, maybe Madras…or Bombay? No language barrier…let me stop with Madras…take stock for a 1,000 rupees…no even 500 should do nicely; I can manage a decent profit each day, just hawking down the streets, with a helper-boy, may be. Otherwise, by the time I turn 60, Chettiyar will pay me 50 per month and what's worse, the same or even more for a newbie rich kid, for doing just nothing!'

'I have 4,000 now. Can't hard work, talent, and divine grace manifold the same to 40,000 or even 400,000?'

'Of course I am risking a stable career, but I no longer fear the consequences on that aspect. If all goes well, I might never need to steal again. If I incur a huge loss, I'll have only myself to blame and seek another job. I am not like Veeran who makes a living out of thieving, farthings at that; and let's face it! Would he let such a bounty pass by? He hasn't been as lucky, so far. Poor Veeran; he must be waiting for me to get him some tea. He's always so proud of me. He wouldn't let me associate with his thievery gang.'

'Brother…! Wonder where he picked that up; but it sounds so good when he calls me that!'

'Brother! Wait, not so fast!' and he'd jump down from the temple car platform, hurrying towards Kumaran.

'Oh brother, I am so glad that you have gained yourself an honourable name, unlike me. Well, where's my tip?' and he would hold out his palm.

Kumaran always saved an anna for Veeran out of his daily allowance of four annas from Chettiyar; even today. As he fished it out of his pocket, lost in thoughts, the clock struck twelve.

'It's a good omen to hear the bells ring. The train to Madras is at 1 pm and tickets will be issued now. I must buy a ticket and head straight to the waiting room. Then, when the train arrives, I'll board as sneakily as possible. Chettiyar would go to the police, of course…or may be, he wouldn't? Could he be slightly indulgent with me who has slogged for him all these years?'

Until he reached the station, got to the ticket counter, handed the 100 rupee note at the counter and asked for a ticket to Madras, his mind kept on chattering steadily and ominously loud for his own comfort.

'Madras?' before the booking clerk could receive the money from him, a hand fell on his shoulder.

'Long journey, brother?'

Now, Kumaran had heard of people dying of cardiac arrests; undergoing one almost, shaken out of his torpor, sweat covering his blanched face, the 100 rupee note slipping out of his fingers, he turned around to face his caller.

It was not a policeman, not Chettiyar, not even Sampath; it was none other than his bosom friend Veeran, smoking a beedi from the corner of his mouth, leaning against a pillar, his eyes scrutinizing the entire station. Kumaran heaved a sigh of relief. Veeran was dressed in a new silk shirt and dhoti.

'Of course, he lives life to the fullest; unlike me, a mere machine.'

'Well, brother, you had me waiting for a long time, only to see you suddenly take the temple route. Completely broke, you were my desperate hope for today; so I began chasing you. But as you kept walking on and on, I realized what you were up to. Well, come along. We'll come back and get your ticket.' Veeran talked with a casual air.

The old man at the booking counter, raised his glasses and peered at both.

'Please don't mind sir, we are friends. What time does the train arrive?'

'12.57.'

'So, there's enough time left, right?'

'Oh yes…plenty,' and he turned to his business.

'Veera…' Kumaran croaked. Lips quivering, his eyes began welling up.

'Idiot? What's all this? Beware of the public. Behave cool and composed as you walk with me.'

'No, Veera. Let me go back to the bank, make the deposit and return to the bank. Please do not tell anybody…' Kumaran entreated his buddy.

Veera guffawed madly. Kumaran shook with even more terror.

'You rogue! You are something, you know? The problem is you're in a dilemma. Don't be. And, if you're leaving, clear all your dues,' smiled Veera.

'Dues? What dues?' blinked Kumaran.

'My tea, sir? Who's going to get me one, starting tomorrow? Today you might as well get me some nice coffee…won't you? Come let's go to that restaurant for a chat,' and he took Kumaran into a fancy cafe within the railway station.

Soon, they were seated in a private room of the cafe, in deep silence.

When the waiter came to their table, Veera cheerfully ordered, 'Today's special dessert please?'

'Veera, I am so scared.'

'Very well, brother! You're talking as if I bid you to do this? Why on earth are you scared of me?'

Kumaran did not reply and hung his head. Tears flowed down his eyes and onto the table mat...

'Brother, you need to be really plucky, more so than being physically strong, for such matters as these. Well, why do you fear me, a rogue myself? Fear the honest man, brother, if there's truly one in this world.'

They stopped short, as the waiter walked in back with their orders. Veera sat imperturbably drumming his fingers on the table, in tune with the music played on the radio.

Veera sampled the *kesari* (saffron flavoured semolina pudding), served by the waiter. Before he could swallow the spoonful, he remembered something and laughed loudly. Kumaran eyed him testily, for his pal's serious lack of empathy, given his own mental state.

'Brother, do you remember? You gave me a long preaching about turning over a new leaf?'

Kumaran recalled the moment and went over what he had said. It was one of Kumaran's bank-errand days and he met Veeran at the temple car. Veeran took his tip and sighed at the money bag in his mate's hands.

'Ah, if only this bounty were in the hands of anyone else...!'

'Well?'

'Well, what? I'd kill for it, if I must… wouldn't I?' and he laughed.

'Veera, you know how much it saddens my heart that you have failed to gain a reputed living? How different is my background from yours? Fundamentally we are of the same class, aren't we?'

'Hey, listen! I am a good-for-nothing loafer. Why waste your time talking to me? But let me tell you one thing. I did not plan to go bad. What started as petty crimes for survival, grew to a stature to make me what I am today. However, I am immensely happy that you, my friend is so virtuous that Chettiyar entrusts you with so much money and responsibility. But let me warn you, there will be tempting times to test the best of men, that calls for the strongest of wills to resist.' And he grew thoughtful as he suddenly exclaimed, a wave of bitter loathing spreading over his face. 'Oh, bother this stinking world and the name it gives you! To hell with it! I know my good and bad. The things I have seen in this world, have roused me enough to kill people by hundreds. Shh, you are running late. Please leave.' And with these words, as Veera fell deeply thoughtful, leaning on the temple car wheel, Kumaran walked away speechless, not taking his eyes off his weird pal, until he turned round the corner of the street.

'Yes, Veera, you were right that day. Nobody aspires to become an outlaw, do they?' and he poured out his coffee.

'Brother, it's natural for all to wish to be virtuous like you. And many succeed in it; because you know, it's not that easy to go vile. You know now! It's simple and easy to stay respectable. However, an easy feat is never profitable. Just think, a good reputation is the only reward for staying honest and good. Your virtues will be praised and taken undue advantage of. Your only gain will be your repute. As long as people are complacent about it, they are virtuous. Well, this is getting too rhetorical. Tell me what are you up to; you are headed for Madras, and then?'

'I have not a clue, Veera...' replied Kumaran staring blankly at the leather money bag.

'Fine, anyone in your position, is in want of some good advice. Listen to me. Your idea of going to Madras is the stupidest of all.'

'Why? Where else can I go?'

'Let me tell you. What time does Chettiyar return to the shop after lunch?' asked Veeran, mentally making some notes, all the while.

'At three in the afternoon.'

'As soon as he's back, he'll send for you at the bank. Right? With no news of you at the bank as well, you can surely imagine what he'd do next?'

'What?'

'He'll file a complaint with the police.'

'Really?'

'Oh no, he'll take a holy dip in the temple pond!' Veeran laughed, brimming with sarcasm.

'No, you know nothing about Chettiyar. He's very diffident towards the police, the courts and those sorts of things; and he has this English-phobia, and hence he keeps away from them as much as possible. Besides, he is a big coward; so he'll let me go as a reward for labouring under him all these years.'

Veera contemplated on what Kumaran said, 'How much is the killing, my brother?'

'Four thousand.'

'What? Four thousand?' Veeran's jaw dropped.

'Well, have no doubt, Chettiyar will go to the police station. When they learn you had left at noon, it will be easy to guess you'd have taken the 1 pm train and all stations in Chennai will be alerted. You'll be arrested right at the Egmore station.'

'Then, what shall be done, mate?' Kumaran pleaded.

'It's the naïve that head straight for Madras, during times as these. You must stay here for at least the next 10 days.'

'Here?'

'Not in this town, but somewhere nearby; say Mayavaram, Cuddalore… and then slowly take it from there, carefully planning the next moves.'

'Veera, I have an idea. Please go with me. Say, whom have you got here? You'll go on gaining a bad name for yourself and nothing else. Let's start a business together and live well. I am sure to get caught if left alone. Please, do come Veera.' Kumaran seized Veera's hand and begged him. However, Veeran was not blind to the undercurrents of his friend's mind—he was obviously wary of letting Veera go back, after learning his secret!

Nevertheless, Veeran pondered over the idea. 'This chap after all these years of a spotless life, in a fit of bravado, is on his way to a new future carrying all this stolen money. If I go with him, and suppose our business ventures fail, we'll have nowhere to go. Of course, I had nothing to lose in the first place, but what of him?' thought he. 'Well, why take such a morbid view of things…and why should I lose this good opportunity?'

The waiter brought their bill. Both fell silent again, as the radio behind them blared loudly.

'Veera, why are you hesitating? Alone, I am sure to get convicted one way or the other. With you beside me, I feel stronger and surer that

I shall never return to my hometown as a convict. Oh, if I must, I will hang myself to death!' Kumaran raved madly.

'Shush! Stop ranting. You shall never return to be a convict.' And he closed his eyes and mused over the idea.

'Veera, please!'

'Well, why all the fuss. I'll go with you,' Veeran rose cheerfully, as Kumaran followed suit.

'Brother, I have an idea. There's a bus, look where it's going.'

'Pondicherry!'

'Well, it's been so long since I boozed, what with this liquor ban here. Let's both go to Pondicherry and then plan our next move from there. What do you say?'

'What have I to say? It's your responsibility from now on. All I ask is save me from trouble. I trust you completely.' As he heard these words, Veeran looked deeply into the eyes of his friend; his expression suddenly changed into a solemn one. His eyes glistened.

'Kumara, say that again, will you?' and he lifted his pal's chin.

'I trust you completely!'

'Oh, you're the first to say these words to me, ever. I never imagined I could be thus trusted by someone,' and he sighed heavily.

'Of course, I shall never betray anyone who trusts me; but I never had a chance to prove that so far,' Veeran told himself.

'Well, come brother. We are off to a new tomorrow!' Veeran put his arm around Kumaran, and gaily walked out of the hotel.

The bus blared loudly and called them towards Pondicherry.

Part II

Kumaran stood by the window of the hotel room, staring mindlessly at the sea.

'Kumara, do you know what drink this is?' Veera joined him, holding up an empty bottle in one hand, a glass of whiskey and a lit cigarette in another.

'I don't know. Leave me alone. I am quite upset!'

'Even I am, brother. Chettiyar must be devastated, right?'

'Well, obviously. After all, it's 4,000. Of course he'd be devastated. But I am more worried about us not getting into trouble.'

'Well, yes. But I didn't mean the money. Chettiyar is affluent enough to let go of this 4,000. He'd be so depressed to learn you've turned dishonest, wouldn't he? Whom could he ever trust again, as he did you?'

Kumaran sighed.

Veera grew tipsy with booze. Dusk fell and as the ocean kept turning golden red, the silvery moon lit the dusky sky.

'Boy!'

The bellboy came running.

'Put two chairs on that balcony facing the sea. Well, Kumara, let's get some fresh sea breeze, shall we?' Slipping his arm around Kumaran's neck, Veeran ushered him over to the balcony. His breath reeked of alcohol, and made Kumaran grimace.

A beautiful cane table and two chairs were placed on the balcony. There were flower pots around. The whiskey glittered gold just as the sky did with the moonlight. A sweet violin melody waffted through the air.

Veeran emptied his glass. His forehead was covered with beads of sweat. Kumaran sat watching him in silence. It seemed his friend had gained several pounds in just one day. Veeran had a strong physique.

'Of course, he'd be. Not everyone is as naïve as I am to care least about themselves. The rogue, making merry out of the money I brought...' And he immediately regretted having brought him along.

'I should have changed my mind as soon as I saw this scoundrel. Why did I have to drag him along in this,' he chided himself.

'Boy!' Veeran called out again to the bellboy.

'Kumaran! You have a drink too, will you? Drinking is not as bad a vice as thieving. What say you, boy?' he addressed the bellboy.

'Of course, sir. Gentlemen like you are known to come and booze here, all the time.'

'Is it so? Do you drink?'

'No, sir!'

'Why not?'

'Never tried.'

'Well, you could. Wait, you rogue! You make a living serving drinks but never touched one? How unfair?'

'Can't afford to, sir. My salary barely makes my ends meet.'

'Oh, please! Please do not talk of misery. I just can't bear that right now...' and he shook his head. Then slowly looked up and asked him kindly.

'What's your name, brother?'

'Vadivelu, sir.'

'And is this your hometown?'

'Yes, sir.'

'What do they pay you here?'

'Fifty rupees, sir.'

'What about your family?'

'My wife, three kids, my parents, and a widowed sister and her two kids; we are ten in all.'

'Are you the sole bread-winner? What of your dad?'

'He is 70, sir, too old to work. He insists though, but I don't have the heart to let him. After all, he's got me, right? I made him swear on me that he wouldn't go looking for work.'

'Vadivelu, Vadivelu...' Veeran put his arm around the bellboy and sobbed. 'You are a great gentleman. The ones who come to your posh hotel to drink only appear so,' and he patted him on his back.

'Sir, do you need anything else?'

'Kumara, what do you say? Would you like a drink?'

'Oh, no. You carry on. I'm fine.'

'Alright, bring me a bottle of beer.'

Once the bellboy left, Veeran asked Kumaran in hushed tones. 'Alright, you don't drink. Have you got any other vices that I do not know of?' And he winked.

'Oh no, I need nothing, and I have got no vices. You're the one born for all that sort of thing,' Kumaran replied testily.

'You have no fun by yourself but envy the one who does. However, one never knows with the likes of you. You might harbour many a secret wish.'

The waiter returned with a beer, and poured it out into a glass mug.

The moon was up now.

'What time is it, now?'

'It's eight, sir.'

'Well, bring our dinner and leave it inside the room.'

'Sir, the bar closes by ten. If you need anything for the night, let me get it for you now.'

'Oh, then please bring a full bottle of brandy or whiskey, two sodas — what time does your shift end?'

'I am done for the day sir. Nine pm…'

'Right Kumara. Do give him his tip,' said Veeran.

'You'll find change in the desk. Please help yourself!' and Kumaran stared into the sky, absent-mindedly.

'Ok, you go and get our dinner,' and Veeran sauntered back to the room and opened the desk. Change? There were fives and tens worth a hundred rupees.

Vadivelu brought back plates with their dinner, as well as the bottles.

'Here Vadivelu!' and Veeran handed him a ten-rupee note. The waiter was puzzled.

'Should I get change, sir?'

'No boy, it's your tip.'

'No, sir. A tip ought to be justified.'

'Oh, you take what I give you. I have the least sense of justice of justification as the world expects. Take this and leave.'

'Sir, I think you are moved, listening to my family's tale. I am not impoverished, sir. My sister earns almost a rupee, daily, by selling idlis.'

Veeran found this even more depressing.

'So, your sister's half-a-rupee income makes you quite well off, does it?' Veeran laughed bitterly.

'Well, it may be nothing to the likes of you. It means quite a lot to me.'

Veeran smiled, marvelling at the transformational effects of money. 'It's much more than what drinking can manage!' he thought.

'Hey listen! Do not delude yourself about my affluence. My plight is worse than yours. Today, I am destined to spend like a king. So I share my good fate with you. If tomorrow, I come to you broke, will you buy me some tea?' Veeran asked him.

'Sir, why do you say such things? You are a wealthy man, God bless!'

'Right, you must see for yourself, to believe it. Here, take this and leave. Kumaran, get up and come here, will you? Let's eat; and then shall we go to the movies?'

Kumaran came and sat inside the room. He remained glum and taciturn. Neither did he ask Veeran anything about the money or Vadivelu's tip. Veeran said nothing either, but he steadily grew testy at his friend's bad-humoured state.

'Hey, what's with you? What need did you have for all this money? You ought to have stayed at work, with your textiles and yardstick. Just so you get more confidence in yourself, you must make an effort and enjoy yourself.'

'Veera, I beg you. Please do not shout, but talk softly,' and he proceeded to shut his pal's mouth with his palm.

With that, Veeran quietly exited the room and stood on the balcony staring at the sea and sky.

Kumaran was agitated and restless. He felt like crying bitterly. He kicked himself for his rash act and bravado. But then, he also felt grateful for Veeran, for he believed his company was better than being alone, going crazy.

'How could I grudge him now? It was I who insisted that he came along. I know nothing about having fun. Why should I envy him, as he says rightly?' Kumaran looked at his friend.

'Veera! Veera, why have you grown silent now. Have I hurt your feelings?' he asked cajolingly.

'If you regret my coming along with you, please say so. I have no problems going back; no hard feelings. What am I to do, if you are not open with me but remain glum all day? I have never had fun all alone. I have left all my companions behind and here you are, in such a bad temper, and cross with me. By now, Marimuthu, Chellan and Raja would be wondering where I was. I hadn't even taken leave of any of them,' and Veera's heart grew heavy in fond memory of his chums.

'Goodness knows, when shall I see them all again?' he sighed.

'Do not worry, Veera. Please forgive me if I have hurt you. What to do, I grew up differently and I am a stranger to your wild ways. You be happy as you are. Come, let's eat,' and he ushered Veera back inside.

'Kumara, shall we go to the movies, after dinner?' Veera turned cheerful once again.

Kumaran did not reply. Neither did he eat much. Veera chattered away happily as he ate. Halfway through the meal, Kumaran got up suddenly and drew closer to the window. His gaze fixed onto a faraway ship amidst the seas, that moved like a small mountain, and whose lights twinkled like stars. He quipped excitedly, 'Veera, I have an idea!'

'What is it?' Veera was busy eating.

'Why don't we board a ship and go to some faraway land? Say, Singapore, Colombo?'

'Oh, certainly, but not now, some 20 years ago. You ignorant fool! It's not that easy to set foot abroad. You must answer a hundred queries at emigration, explain the money you take along. Can you?' Veera replied, washing his hands.

'Oh, I see!' Kumaran rubbed his forehead.

'Brother…why do you worry unnecessarily? It's my responsibility to make sure no harm comes to you. We are here for a couple of days to chill-out and plan things. This is a safe hide-out. You are constantly worrying, though.' Fully drunk, Veeran's eyes were red and his words faltered a bit.

'Alright, I am going out. You want to come?' Veeran lit a cigarette.

'No, I am going to bed.'

'Alright, good night. Give me some money, will you?'

'Why do you ask me? You can take all you want…' Kumaran was unreasonably annoyed with even money per se, and too disgusted to open the money bag and look into it.

Veeran opened the desk and picked up a few notes and coins and thrust them into his pocket. 'Keep the money bag safe under your pillow while you sleep,' he instructed Kumaran, and combed his hair, looking at the mirror.

'Must you go out, for sure?' asked Kumaran who was already in bed.

'Damn! Will you let me do anything at all?' Said Veeran and he threw the comb on the floor. He was clearly annoyed now.

'Please don't get angry Veera. I am afraid to stay here alone, that's why.'

'Oh, fear nothing. There are folks in other rooms as well. Let me lock the room and take the key with me. You sleep well. Rest assured, and be happy that all your troubles are over now. Bye for now.' As Veeran locked the room and climbed down the steps, he heard Kumaran calling out, 'Don't be long!'

'Alright!'

A man seated at the hotel reception watched him curiously as he left the building. Veeran however did not notice as he whistled merrily and went on his way.

The streets were wide and long. The sea could be heard roaring loudly in the stillness of the night. The moonlight was intoxicating to say the least.

A cycle rickshaw drew closer and stopped near him. Veeran got in and seated himself.

'Where, sir?'

'Anywhere!'

'Sure sir!' replied the rickshaw rider cheerfully, as he pedalled the rickshaw. The rickshaw trotted along the long street, and vanished round the corner. Just as it turned the corner, engaged in small talk with the driver, Veeran burst out laughing, his mirth echoing in its wake.

Part III

At 1 pm that night, the rickshaw returned to the hotel. A fully drunk Veeran got down, rummaged through his pocket and handed the driver some rupee notes randomly.

The rickshaw driver counted the notes in the moonlight. There were nine one-rupee notes in all.

'Good night sir. I'll see you tomorrow morning!' and he gladly took leave. Too tipsy to talk, waving his hands madly, Veeran entered the hotel. The bellboy who was lying on the porch, woke up and switched on the staircase lights. The clerk who had sat working at the reception desk when Veeran had left, still sat working. Veeran turned to look at him. The man must be over 50, his hair grey. He looked back at Veeran through his glasses. His eyes were bloodshot from lack of sleep.

'Poor man. Such hard work to make ends meet….'

'Hello sir!'

'Hello…'

'How much do they pay you for such slogging day and night?'

The clerk found this impertinent but he replied, '100 rupees.'

'Big family?'

He laughed… 'Yes.'

'Are you able to manage?'

'Not quite, but what can I do?'

'Oh…the world is not as it should be,' Veeran shook his head.

'Okay, sir. Good night. See you in the morning.'

'I never talk in the morning. Not the truth, even if I do. Do not mistake this for a drunkard's prattle. Let me ask you something; answer me honestly. Have you ever experienced life with such ultimate bliss that the heavens were here? Tell me, sir.'

The clerk thought for a moment. He realized that Veeran was not merely ranting but he was mildly surprised. Also, Veeran's appearance — silk shirt and hairstyle — rendered him suspicious. However, he proceeded to reply.

'Oh yes…' He looked at the mirror on the wall. 'I was 20. Clara was my classmate and she had accepted my proposal. We were to be married in 10 days. Soon after our engagement, we used to meet in the park. Those days, the world and everything in it was so beautiful and heavenly. Soon it came to nothing.'

Veeran laughed.

'You are right. It must have been so. So how long did your paradise last? And then what happened and why?'

'Money! If only we had had a little more of it, we could have saved our paradise a little.'

'Of course! Money cannot create heavens. But the lack of it can take you to hell. Poverty and hunger leads humans to a life of unspeakable humiliation and misery. They are born just once, and some die getting nothing ever out of life except all its agonies. Oh, such poor souls; this world is nothing as it should be, nothing…' crying his heart out, Veeran climbed up the steps.

Sauntering along the way, he reached their room, opened the locked door and switched on the light. Kumaran hadn't slept. He was sitting on the bed, his head resting on his crossed knees. Veeran felt sorry for him but was also annoyed.

He knew it was useless to deal with him kindly anymore. 'Hey Kumaran. Come here this moment,' he growled.

Kumaran trembled with fear.

'What do you mean by staying awake so late?'

'I can't sleep; I am so disturbed,' Kumaran could have cried.

'Just you wait!' and he picked up the brandy bottle from the table, opened the seal and poured out two glasses with soda. 'Here, drink up. You'll be fine. Come on, drink it up.'

'No, please. I'll go to sleep right now,' Kumaran lay down and covered himself with his blanket.

'No way. You must drink. I'll see to it. Here, hold this,' and he thrust a glass in Kumaran's hands, who took it with disgust and fear wrought across his face.

Veeran who had emptied his glass by now, had his eyes welling up. About a minute later, his face convulsed and lips quivered. He began sobbing uncontrollably, covering his face. 'Kumara, this world is not what it should be, brother. Man, woman, and their children, their woes—it's too much to bear,' Veeran shook his head and wept like a child.

Kumaran was utterly perplexed. Was that Veeran crying? He could not believe his eyes.

'Veera, what happened? I never imagined you were so tender-hearted. Why are you crying?' he asked worriedly.

'Kumara—I am not weeping for myself but this world. I always do; you have seen me at it tonight.' Tears kept flowing from his eyes.

'What do you mean you always weep? We've heard only your roaring laughs and joyous chatter!'

'It's just a façade, Kumara! Deep inside I harbour great sorrows and I perpetually weep. Do you know, there's an inner person within each of us?'

'What?'

'Yes, the meekest fellow has an inner person who's always imagining the cruellest of horrors to mete out to others. What you hold in your hands has the ability to bring him out. The truth will be out, and that's the reason the worst of cowards commit the worst of crimes when drunk. And people drink to come to terms with that inner self, to let out that secret person. I see wretched people, and weep for them bitterly, involuntarily; what to do, my inner self is such a tender coward, I guess...' heaving another sob, Veeran wiped his eyes.

'What's the misery you saw right now, to make you weep so?'

'Miseries! What else does one happen to see in this world?' And he closed his eyes and leaned back on his chair.

Within his shut eyes, loomed a vision. Hundreds of hungry hounds with pitiful faces and expectant eyes, panting and drooling for a morsel to eat. Soon the dogs fade, and their place is taken by hundreds of children, their eyes physically so different from that of the dogs, yet the expression, just the same, their weak hands outstretched...and behind them, hundreds of women, and the horrors they undergo for the sake of a few pennies...

'Oh, how did this all come to happen? Why is the world thus fallen?' He could bear the thought no longer. He sobbed again bitterly.

Kumaran had heard of people emoting a lot when drunk. Also, he was intrigued by what Veeran had said about people wanting to allow free rein to their inner selves. He found himself wanting that as well. 'So what, if I take a small drink. It's not as if it's going to make things any worse than now.'

'Veera! It saddens my heart to see you weep so. What good can come out of you or me crying for this world, however terrible it may be. Alright, must I drink this?' he held out the glass.

'Yes, my dear! Only then will you be my brother in the real sense.'

'Why does it smell so strange?' and he sniffed the drink. 'Oh, what's this odour! Odour? It's not that bad…actually it smells like biscuits,' and he brought the glass to his lips.

'Yes! There you are. Take a gulp! Well done!' Veeran patted Kumaran's back. They opened a packet of biscuits and filled their glasses again.

'How do you feel? Giddy?' asked Veera.

'Hmm…I feel nothing,' Kumaran pursed his lips.

'Alright, have some more.' And he added a little more to Kumaran's glass, who drank up readily. He felt his throat sting, but otherwise he felt nothing.

'Well, Veera, I don't see my inner fellow anywhere about, as you said!'

'Patience, brother. The one who's just left, you will fetch him from within,' Veera laughed, and then remembering something he said, 'Poor girl, she!'

'Which girl?'

'I met somebody a while ago.'

'Oh yeah, you pity her, but still you slept with her!'

'Well, how else is one to help her, anyway?'

'Oh, come on! It was her choice, and a bad and gutsy one. Should you weep for her too? Did she find no honourable means to live?'

'Brother Kumara! Had you no honourable means to live, with a roof atop and three meals a day? Yet, what have you done now?'

'What have I done?'

'Very well, do you at least recognize me now?'

'Oh do you mean the money I have looted? You have no right to say a word about it. I stole it and it's my money. You have no claims to it or even talk of it...but I might.' Kumaran's tone had hardened and his words faltered.

'Yes, brother! It's your money indeed. I ask for no share in it, but let me partake in your sin. I gave you the courage to come this far; else you might have gone back anytime. Kumara, pardon me. It's I who has ruined you,' and he held Kumaran's hands and wept.

'Why do you weep? You want to partake in my sins? Take all of them,' and he flopped on to the bed, his arms widespread.

Veeran kept weeping all night, brooding long over all the sins and woes of humankind.

Kumaran who lay on the bed, suddenly felt his head throb. He felt a renewed vigour take hold of him and his nerves tingling. All of a sudden, he jumped out of his bed, bursting out into laughter.

Veeran was stupefied at Kumaran's sudden and strange display of mirth.

'Hey Veera, Chetty is fooled! Serves him right. How dare he pay me 30 a month, and that idiot Sampath the same? Serves him right. You

know how he has thrashed me? Hey Veera, come let's go and set fire
to his shop someday. Oh you're a coward. You wouldn't go. You are
a coward who knows only to weep!' With these words he fell on the
bed, still laughing.

'Kumara, please don't say such things. Chettiyar is a good man. He
trusted you so much. Don't curse him. After all, we are making merry
at his cost, aren't we?'

'Oh, come on! The money is mine. Are you here to keep reminding me
it's his money? It's my money, MINE!' screamed Kumaran.

Kumaran's loud shrieks and laughs woke up the guests in the adjacent
rooms. One of them knocked at their door and politely called out
through their window. 'Mister...mister...'

'Who's that?' Kumaran retorted arrogantly.

'I stay in the next room, sir. It is past 2 am. It would be nice if you could
keep your voice down. We want to sleep.'

'Nonsense, if you want to sleep, go elsewhere. This is a place to party.
I'll shout all I want. Oh yeah! Chettiyar is a fool. I fooled him! The
4,000 is all mine!' Kumaran's loud voice could be heard streets away.

'Kumara, will you keep it quiet please?' Veeran tried to shut his mouth
with his palm.

Kumaran pushed him aside, 'What for you, idiot? It's my money.
I shall speak about it.'

'That's all very well, brother. Remember we must go and buy stock
tomorrow for our business. Let's go to bed so we can rise early.'

'Hey! Look who's talking like a big merchant! You scoundrel, you
might be planning to run away looting my money while I'm asleep,
for all I know.'

'Brother! Do you suspect me? Can I do such a thing to you? Have you ever heard of me betraying my trusted ones?' Veeran shed tears, again.

'Well, have you ever heard of me running away with Chettiyar's money? Well, here I am, right? What makes you different?'

By then most of the other guests woke up and came to see what the commotion was all about. Hearing the noise, the reception clerk and the bellboys came up running too.

'Hey, is that the bellboy? We need another bottle of brandy here. Could you get us one?' Kumaran asked him through the window.

'No sir, the bar shuts at ten. I can get you drinks at six in the morning,' the bellboy replied.

'If money is your concern, have no worries. The guests in your other rooms are beggars compared to me. Here, ask them to show me such a bounty as this!' and he pulled the money bag from beneath the pillow, opened it and held out the stack of notes for everyone to see.

Flabbergasted, Veeran watched his friend's antics in silence.

One of the guests and the hotel's clerk put their heads together, and discussed something deeply in hushed tones.

The guest said, 'Sir, please call the police. These boys are surely up to no good. And their appearances are anything but honourable.'

'Not now. Soon, they'll collapse. I shall summon the police, then.'

'Hey saint, who weeps for the world! Please do so for the idiotic Chettiyar as well!'

Veeran made a potion with some kind of drug from his pockets, got Kumaran to drink it and put him to bed.

Exhausted, they lay helter skelter in deep slumber — Kumaran on the bed, and Veeran on one of the chairs.

As the clock struck five, a police van arrived at the hotel. The clerk led the inspector and constables to the boys' room.

The inspector tapped on the door with his stick. Veeran woke hearing the sounds and looked through the window.

'Police!'

'Oh yes, it's the police, open the door!'

Veeran quietly went to the door and opened it. The policemen entered the room.

'Hey, are you Kumaran, who works at the Chettiyar's textile shop?'

'No sir, that's him.'

'Hey, wake up, will you?' The inspector tapped on the sleeping Kumaran's shoulder. Kumaran woke up and on seeing the policemen, immediately fell at their feet and sobbed, 'Sir, it's not me, it's him!'

He was sober now. Veeran smiled to himself.

He remembered Kumaran's words 'You want to partake in my sins? Take all of it!'

He also remembered how he pleaded and placed his trust on him… 'I trust you completely!'

'Kumara, say that again, will you? …I shall never betray anyone who trusts me; but I never had a chance to prove that so far.' How he had sighed contentedly at being his pal's trusted confidante.

'…I shall never return to my hometown as a convict. Oh, if I must, I shall hang myself!'

'…You shall never return to be a convict.'

Veeran went over the events of the previous day and their talks.

He was truly glad to hear Kumaran blaming him.

The inspector took a long look at Veeran. He was quick to see what a ruffian he was.

'Hey you, what did you do to this lad? How did you bring him here?' and he hit him hard twice below the knee.

'Sir, I'll tell all. Don't hit me please!' Veeran screamed in pain.

'Hmm, out with it!' growled the inspector.

'Sir, I'll tell you everything,' and he began spinning a clever tale of lies. 'Sir, this fellow's the most honest in our village, but he's a friend of mine. On his way to the bank, he takes me out for tea, as a routine. Yesterday as we were having tea, I eyed his money bag, and mixed this drug in his tea. When he was half-conscious, I dragged him onto a bus and brought him here,' and he showed the inspector the drug he had in his pockets.

'Once he gained consciousness, I kept him threatened, with this knife, so he couldn't shout for help. There, I have told you all. Please don't hit me.' He folded his hands and pleaded.

Hitting him squarely on the back of his neck, the inspector handed Veeran over to a constable and turned to Kumaran.

'You seem alright. Why do you keep such bad company? Look what trouble it has landed you in, now? Thank goodness, your boss Chettiyar had given a complaint that you must have been beaten and looted.' Kumaran hung his head down and kept weeping quietly. He looked up at Veeran and begged for pardon with beseeching eyes.

'It's quite alright, what you did,' Veeran's eyes smiled in reply.

Finally, as he was about to leave from the police station, Kumaran went up to Veeran who was now in the lock-up. Eyes filled with tears of chagrin, Kumaran choked for words, 'Veera, you are a great martyr!'

'Oh, no brother. This is not a big deal for me. You have nothing great to thank me. In fact I am being a little selfish here.'

'What are you saying, Veera?'

'Oh yes, if you turn into a convict and accompany me to jail, who'll get me some tea when I am released? I need someone, right?' Veeran laughed.

Part IV

As was his routine, Kumaran stopped for a moment at the temple-car platform on his way to the bank.

'Brother, you seem not to have noticed me!' He could almost hear Veeran's voice and his eyes welled up.

'It will be a year until he's back.' He sighed.

One of the fruit-sellers, an old woman, said to Kumaran, 'Dear lad, you're lucky to be back alive. Oh yes, he's a treacherous convict. We always used to wonder what this good lad had to do with such a scoundrel. See what he's done to you. Thank goodness, you are safe,' and she wiped her eyes with empathy.

Likewise, Chettiyar, the little boy, even Sampath had embraced Kumaran and wept.

'Never mind the money. I was so worried about your safety...' and he cursed Veeran loud and long.

Whenever he thought of Veeran or when he passed by his hangouts, now deserted, Kumaran recollected his voice, his laughter and couldn't help his eyes welling up.

'The one who wept for this world is condemned by the world. Do I weep for him now? Do I deserve to? Not only me, but nobody does. Hey, foolish world! He weeps for you, and you weep for me. Of course, when have you ever opened your eyes to the truth? Weep for the liar. Weep for me! Weep just for me!'

Talking to himself bitterly, Kumaran went on his way.

Translator's Note

The stories in this collection have been randomly picked from the author's works over a period of years. What they have in common is my ardent liking for each of them. These have been handpicked for reasons best known to my heart, though I shall try putting it in words to the best of my ability.

Jayakanthan, or JK as he's fondly known, is best known for his ability to explore a myriad of sensitive emotions in human relationships; especially of women. The self-talk of his women characters is incredibly authentic and relatable, accounting for his wide fan base of women.

I have enjoyed reading and re-reading these stories as a teen and still do; I have also chosen them for the same reason—they are timeless classics in terms of literary value, quite engaging at that.

Acknowledgements

I would like to thank all those who believed in me and saw me through this book, and gave me all the support and encouragement I needed. Of those, first comes Dr Rudhran (psychiatrist), who planted the idea in my mind in 2014, with sincere words that acted as the prime mover for this project.

My dear Amma, a woman I admire for her sheer emotional strength, the way she carried herself with dignity through an extraordinary life, and her unconditional belief in the best of her loved ones.

My dear Mami, companion of my father for more than 50 years, who instilled in me a lot of delightful interests, including reading and writing.

My nicer and wiser half Joe, whose love and support sees me through everything, and who constantly reminds me to believe more in myself. My dear sister Ammu, who loves me unconditionally and inspires me constantly.

My heartfelt gratitude goes to Preeti Gill, as well as Dr Bhattacharjee and Priyamvada of Niyogi Books for helping me publish this book, my first one at that!

My special and much endeared thanks would be for my dear friend, mentor, and revered author Ambai, for the insightful introduction, and for being my constant motivator and ruthlessly honest critic!

Last but not the least, thank you dear reader, for picking up this book. I hope you find it a good read!

The stories in chronological order of publication

It's Only Words 1960

Beyond Cognizance 1961

A Friend Indeed 1962

The Crucifixion 1962

The Pallbearers 1962

The Guilty 1963

The Truth 1963

The Heroine 1964

The Pervert 1964

New Horizons 1965

The Masquerade (a novelette) 1962